Calico Kids

By Todd Downing

FIRST EDITION

ISBN: 978-1-7349293-2-4

Copyright © 2019 Todd Downing & Deep7 Press

All Rights Reserved Worldwide

Edited by Dan Heinrich, Raechelle Downing, & Andrea Edelman

Cover design by Todd Downing

WWW.TODDDOWNING.COM

Romeo Void – *Fear to Fear*
(Iyall / Zincavage / Woods / Bossi)
© ® Talk Dirty Music / BMI

Lyrics used by permission

Deep7 Press is a subsidiary of Despot Media, LLC
1214 Woods Rd SE Port Orchard, WA 98366 USA
WWW.DEEP7.COM

To the old gang,
some of whom are still alive,
much to everyone's surprise
(perhaps most of all our own)

Foreword

Once upon a time...

No, wait. That makes it sound as if this never happened.

I mean, it *didn't* happen, but it also sorta *did*.

In the olden days before the Internet and mobile phones and helicopter parents, a lot of kids—especially those of middle-class working folks—ran wild, left to their own devices from the end of the school day until dinner time, and often beyond then, especially on weekends. I was among that generation of "latchkey kids", *Generation X* as we've become known. Sandwiched between the Baby

Boomers and Millennials like processed Oscar Meyer lunchmeat. And I have to admit, if we must be tagged with a generational moniker, I can think of nothing better than to carry the namesake of Billy Idol's post-*Chelsea* punk band.

I spent the years between ages eight and sixteen in the sleepy seaside community of Aptos, California, tucked at the north end of Monterey Bay, about an hour's drive south of San Francisco. At the time, it was populated by artists and hippies and the various blue-collar and white-collar wage slaves that make up any American small town. If a parent worked in tech or a large industry, chances are it required an hour commute "over the hill" into what would come to be called Silicon Valley.

In the late '70s and early '80s, when such communities only had *broadcast* television and *land lines*, we kids spent a lot of time in our heads. We gathered in small gangs—I'm still not sure if the technical term is a *gaggle* or a *murder*—riding our bikes all over town like two-wheeled hellions, spending our meager allowances on drugstore candy and comic books, dumping the rest in the arcade machines, and generally living life without a helmet.

I'm not trying to romanticize the experience. Multiple skateboarding and cycling accidents, three concussions, and almost being drowned in the high school swimming pool by a bully twice my size may have built some character, but it also left some very real scars. Life without a helmet, or whatever analog you wish to use, is strictly subjective. Like everything, it had its good bits and its bad bits, and gave everyone lucky enough to survive some entertaining stories, and plenty of baggage to sort through.

Truly, a gift that keeps on giving.

In the summer of 1982, I was fourteen years old. I had a small circle of best friends with whom I spent every spare moment of the day, playing Atari, riding our bikes to Beer Can Beach, or climbing the railroad trestles like insane monkeys. Our uniform was a pullover hoodie, Levis or OP shorts, and usually either Vans or Nikes on our feet. Our vehicles were self-propelled and often home-built hybrids. The last twenty minutes of *E.T.*, when the boys are outrunning the feds on their bikes? That was us.

We played epic, marathon sessions of *Dungeons & Dragons,* got my buddy's single mom to get us into rated-R movies, and experimented with beer and weed in the safety of an older friend's apartment. We went on weekend camp-outs in Nisene Marks National Forest, and counted the days until our sixteenth birthday, when we could level up for real with a driver's license.

In writing *Calico Kids*, I wanted to give the reader a sort of urban fantasy adventure—or rural fantasy—but couch everything in very real history. So although the riverside community of Calico is fictional, it's not quite a wholesale invention. It's somewhat as if I picked up Aptos, California in the summer of 1982, and set it down on the north bank of the Rogue River in southwestern Oregon.

The dictionary definition of *nostalgia* is a sentimental longing or wistful affection for the past, which is not my intent. This is not a memoir, or a treatise on how awesome growing up in the 1980s was, because it frequently was *not*. (Ever-present doom cloud of nuclear annihilation? Thanks! I'll have mine to-go.) It is simply a setting and a period with which I'm intimately familiar. And as my English professors always told me, "write what you know."

At the end of the day, I wouldn't change my life without a helmet. But I wouldn't necessarily recommend it, either. It was a crazy, chaotic time, full of dizzying highs and tragic lows, and monsters around every corner—not for the faint of heart. I applaud everyone who came through that time without the privilege my friends and I had. Well done indeed.

- Todd Downing, Port Orchard, WA
  Summer, 2020

A Few Things

Chapters are given a song title, along with the artist and year of release. Think of it as a mix-tape of sorts. In addition, I've created a curated playlist on Spotify as a sort of inspirational "soundtrack". You can find the link at:

www.todddowning.com/calico-kids

Immense gratitude to Debora Iyall of Romeo Void for permission to use the lyric from *Fear to Fear*.

Likewise, my thanks to Dan Heinrich, Trish Heinrich, Rob Lowry, Malcolm Collie, Julie Collie, Allan McComas, Raffael Boccamazzo, and Ron Dugdale, for beer and inspiration.

Tip of the hat to Mark Bruno and James Stubbs, who wrote the Boomtown Calico setting for my *Six Gun* RPG.

Thanks also to Jeff Antonio and Christian Zabala of NBC Universal and Universal Music Group, respectively.

Babciu is a Polish term of endearment for grandmother and is roughly pronounced "bob-chew".

Content warning: bullying, substance use/abuse, occult & supernatural themes.

Track 1:

OUR TOWN

Kim Wilde (1980)

The digital clock in the Soundesign cassette deck blinked over to 7:30 a.m., and Blue Öyster Cult's *Burnin' For You* erupted from the tiny pair of speakers beneath the faux-wood case. A soft breeze blew in off the river, bidding the decades-old flower-print curtains dance to the song, carrying the competing odors of pulp mill and salmon cannery to the nostrils of the slumbering teenage boy.

A.J. stirred at the sudden assault of smells and power chords, and reached for his glasses on the milk crate nightstand. Contorting into a semi-reclining position, he grabbed the clock and turned it toward him, yawning.

Alan Jennings was small for his age—thirteen among peers who were already fourteen and dating. What his dad called "shit-brown" eyes squinted through an unruly mop of dishwater blond hair, bangs kept long to hide the acne on his forehead. His left cheek was already pitted from a fishing accident when he was eight; the hook was still somewhere in his tackle box.

Had he really set his alarm for 7:30? Sure, the extra half hour of sleep was badly needed after studying into the wee hours, but...7:30? Was he insane?

A.J. was a good student. He was also short, skinny, far-sighted, and thus a target for harassment of every type imaginable. Being a font of local history and at least three or four juicy conspiracy theories didn't help matters. But he was scrappy and fast, and used humor as a finely-honed weapon. Or at least he used to, before he got on Liam's good side. This year had actually been bearable due to the bully's protection. Seventh grade the previous year had been a living hell. What had begun as a protection-for-homework arrangement had blossomed into a legitimate friendship, bonding over cultural staples of hard rock and *Dungeons & Dragons*.

A.J. jumped from his bed and pulled a three-day-old pair of Levis over scrawny, pale legs. It was Friday of finals week, with just four days left in the school year, including today. For A.J., that meant graduation from Calico Junior High ("Go Herons!") and entering as a freshman at Calico High ("Go Lumberjacks!"). He shrugged into a *Star Wars* logo tee and a red flannel shirt with a selection of mechanical pencils in the chest pocket. His socks were the only article of clothing clean from the drawer.

Hopping out of his bedroom and down the hall, he tried to wrestle his feet into a pair of leather Nikes from last year. At one time, they'd been white, with a red "swoosh" on the side. But now they were a sort of sad gray, tinged with brown, rubber soles ground down to zero tread, seams and edges worn and ragged. The shoes barely fit, but he knew he could look forward to some school clothes money from Gram this summer.

The small Craftsman bungalow on Ash Street was quiet and empty, his parents having left for work at least thirty minutes ago, mom to open the Val-U Drug she managed on Third, dad to Lynx & Co. Construction at Fourth and Lamont, where he toiled as an accountant.

Plucking a foil pack of two Pop Tarts from the box on the kitchen table, A.J. grabbed his jacket and backpack from the corner behind the door and ran into the wide world outside. Still groggy from the late-night cram session, he pulled his Huffy Thunder Road BMX bike from the side of the wood pile under the eaves of the carport and saddled up in a single, well-practiced motion. Letting gravity give him an extra burst of speed down the hill, A.J.

lowered his head into the late spring breeze and sped toward the road to school.

He had an algebra test in first period, and he was late.

Calico, Oregon was a small, blue collar community of four thousand rugged individuals, nestled on the north bank of the Rogue River, less than five miles due east of Gold Beach. Originally a mining boomtown in the 1850s (named for colorful silver prospector "Calico" Jim Broughton), a mine explosion and gas cloud in 1882 had made the old site unlivable, forcing the residents to move a couple of miles down river.

A.J. dropped down from Hill Avenue onto the bottom half of Hillcrest Drive, which became Lamont Street as it intersected with Fourth Avenue, bordered with flower boxes and bike racks. The aroma from the Golden Palace Chinese restaurant hung in the morning air, the iconic trademark of the oldest continually-owned business in town. His route was so etched in his brain that he could ride it blindfolded, as long as there wasn't any other traffic.

South on Lamont, left on Pioneer past the dental office and lumber company, where vibrant banners lining the street reminded residents of the upcoming town centennial in August. Then a right onto Silver Street, which ran alongside the school's athletic field. Dave's Deli at Third and Silver was a popular sandwich shop for junior high students walking off-campus for lunch, at least students with cash to spend—unlike A.J.

He knew a fair amount of local history, how Calico had reinvented itself as a respectable logging community after the re-charter. The access road he now used as a shortcut to school hadn't seen a truck in over a decade; most deliveries to the pulp mill usually arrived on the river frontage road. The pulp mill had been the primary employer here since 1920, followed by the fish cannery on the west side of town. Most other businesses—from the diners to the real estate office, the bars to the auto garage on Third Avenue—supported the mill and cannery workers and their families. They also employed wives and teenagers. When he turned fourteen, he'd be able to get a work permit and a part-time gig somewhere. His mom would likely push him toward stocking shelves at the Val-U Drug, but he was far more interested in Dave's, or the ice cream parlor on Cantor Street, for the obvious fringe benefit of free food.

A.J.'s stomach growled. The cold Pop Tarts had done nothing to assuage his hunger, and their calories had all but burned away on the ride.

He approached Calico Junior High at high speed and found Kristof Korolewski already locking his bike to one of the stalls out front. Kris was fourteen and a first-generation American, his Polish family having immigrated to the States after World War Two. He was blond and apple-cheeked, and a good half-foot taller than A.J.

The Korolewskis owned and operated the Silver City Diner on Second and Durham, complete with a small "arcade", which was really just an old coat check room crammed with *Space Invaders, Asteroids,* and *Pac-Man* cabinets, a blurry Sportsman duck hunting game, and an Evel Knievel pinball machine from 1977. The diner even featured an old grandmother who spoke fractured English and had a milky eye, but who made the most amazing *pierogi* ever tasted within a hundred miles of Curry County.

Kris worked the weekday dinner shift and occasional weekend mornings, and was never without a ready supply of those very meat and vegetable dumplings. He tended to use them to buy the friendships in his life, which was really unnecessary. He was a good kid to begin with.

"Hey Kris," A.J. hailed as he skidded to a halt, dismounting the banana seat like a cowboy in an old western. He pulled the front wheel into the rack space next to Kris and undid the combination lock without even looking at it. He could see their friend Liam's "Frankenbike" opposite their own cycles, a patchwork of primer-gray aluminum, cannibalized black BMX parts, and a seat held together with duct tape.

"You're late," Kris joked, knowing full well they were in the same algebra class, and would share the same fate for being tardy.

A.J. glanced down at "the Kricyle"—an old Schwinn cruiser with knobby tires, advertising placard in the center frame, and a milk crate basket at each end for delivering take-out to the local community. "Up late too?"

"No doubt," Kris answered, adjusting the strap of his backpack on his left shoulder. "Gotta ace this final or hello, summer school."

"Your folks wouldn't do that to you," A.J. dismissed with a wave. "They need you at the diner."

The two boys left the long rack of Huffy street bikes, Schwinn BMX conversions, and Raleigh Choppers, heading toward homeroom and their math final.

"Besides," A.J. said, playfully slugging his larger friend in the shoulder, "you've got this."

Track 2:
STORIES FOR BOYS

U2 (1980)

By lunchtime the news had filtered over from the high school: Jeannie Wells hadn't shown up for classes, and hadn't come home last night. Ordinarily, gossip of this kind would have slipped past them. The high school sophomore was popular, full of school spirit, and considered attractive by her peers —all things A.J.'s gang weren't. However Calico was a small American town, and as with most small American towns, connections ran like a nervous system beneath the surface.

Jeannie's parents had been close with A.J.'s at one time, so close that they'd been asked to be his godparents. Three years ago, a brain aneurysm had claimed Sally Wells, leaving David Wells to soldier on alone, raising his teenage daughter and splitting his time between the paper mill and Elliott's bar two blocks away. A.J.'s family hardly saw David

Wells anymore. And Jeannie had withdrawn into her very specific social circle, sighted less frequently than Sasquatch by A.J. and his ilk. Despite her tragic family situation, Jeannie was known as a good girl and a straight-A student, so it was highly newsworthy that she hadn't returned the previous night.

Liam approached the outdoor picnic table and A.J. braced for a noogie that never came. He would have taken it, gladly, just to be reminded of what he was avoiding by being under the protection of William "Liam" Scott. Hidden beneath a camo Army jacket three sizes too big, Liam was six feet and 150 pounds of the kind of coiled muscle only seen on skinny, under-nourished kids who lifted weights. The fourteen-year-old hadn't picked up the shaving habit yet, so scraggly black hairs jutted randomly from his mouth and chin. An uncombed mass of curly, dark hair fell forward over a pair of mirrored aviators, which hid ever-wary chestnut eyes. His ruddy complexion spoke of Shasta and Coquille ancestry somewhere back, a notion he was the first to reaffirm with tales of his mother's alcoholism, mostly so no one else could bring it up first.

But today was not to be about drunk mother stories. Today was all about the disappearance of a local celebrity.

"You hear about Jeannie?" Liam asked.

Kris joined them, producing a paper lunch sack from his backpack. "In gym, they were talking about finding her body in the creek out by Old Town."

A.J. rolled his eyes. "Bullshit. The rumors are getting out of hand."

"That's what rumors do," Liam grunted.

"What do you think happened?" Kris threw a quizzical glance at Liam, opening a smaller paper bag full of *pierogi* and offering them to the erstwhile bully.

Liam took a handful of small Polish dumplings and ate them one by one as he pondered. "You know Jeannie's dating Eric Somerville…"

"Yeah," Kris nodded, "they're always hanging out at the diner."

A.J. squinted. "Were they there last night?"

"Sure. They each had a Coke and shared a basket of fries—"

"I wasn't asking what they ordered," A.J. sighed.

Liam grabbed A.J.'s can of Rondo and took a swig. "They probably went up to The Bluff to park."

Kris and A.J. exchanged a look that was somewhere between jealousy and bewilderment. Neither had been on a date, much less "parked"—that was an activity reserved for high school kids—but both were a little curious, and growing more curious by the month. Indian Bluff was a well-known spot favored by teens with access to four-wheeled vehicles and later curfews. It was a turnout on an old logging spur from North Bank Rogue River Road, overlooking the site of Old Calico and the adjacent clearcut. Although "The Bluff" was shielded by forest to the west, sunsets bathed the ghost town in beautiful hues of pink and orange, almost an incentive to stop making out for five minutes and bask in nature's glory.

"How do you know?" Kris asked.

Liam shrugged. "I don't. Not for sure. But ever since Eric got that Nova running, they've been going up there a lot."

"We should look for them," A.J. blurted. It was more forceful than he'd intended.

Liam raised his eyebrows behind the glasses and chuckled. "Okay, hotshot. Just how do you figure we go about this?"

"We should go by Jeannie's house first," A.J. replied. "Check on Mr. Wells. He works the swing shift at the mill, so he might still be home when we get there."

"If we meet at the diner," Kris added, "I can have *Babciu* make some fresh *pierogi* to take over."

Their plan was foolproof. The three boys had all arranged to take a 7th-period prep this semester. Kris actually had a legitimate reason, as he worked after school at the diner, but Liam and A.J. followed suit, and on days when Liam wasn't in detention, it meant an early start on activities like playing *Dungeons & Dragons* at A.J.'s, fishing at their secret spot up the river, or besting one another's high score on *Pac-Man* at the diner.

After a quick stop to pick up Kris and a fresh bag of *pierogi*, they saddled up and pedaled to the outskirts of town, where a small manufactured home sat on a shy acre of wooded land. A.J. had been here many times prior to the death of Mrs. Wells, not so much in the past couple years.

Mr. Wells' red Chevy pickup was nowhere to be seen.

The three boys shared a conspiratorial look, and without a word, walked their bikes around to the back door, which had been left unlocked as Liam immediately found by testing the handle.

"Nobody's home, guys," Kris observed.

"Yeah, no shit, Sherlock," Liam scowled. "We're just gonna see if there are any clues to where Jeannie might be, leave the *pierogi* and a note."

A.J. shivered but refused to show his nerves. "What are you worried about?" he asked, following Liam inside.

"Aside from prosecution for B&E, nothing," Kris retorted, looking at the greasy bag of food in his left hand before taking a deep breath and following the other two boys.

Liam was already explaining the related legal technicalities to Kris as they crept inside. "There's no 'B', because the door was unlocked. No breaking. Just entering."

"Trespassing, at most," A.J. added, gazing around the interior.

The home was dim from the aluminum blinds covering the windows, turned closed. Avocado shag carpet held the smell of cigarettes and winter mildew. A.J. thought the place could use some airing out.

While Kris took a lookout position at the kitchen bar, setting the bag on a counter of mottled yellow Formica, Liam and A.J. crept quietly down the hall to the bedrooms. Mr. Wells' door was open and revealed a dark, disheveled room beyond: the bedclothes were a jumbled mass, mingled with the laundry pile, empty beer bottles littering the nightstands and floor. It smelled like the family room where they'd entered the house, with the addition of adult male body odor. Wells worked a physical job, so it was to be expected that his sleeping area would harbor that scent.

Jeannie's bedroom door was closed, but none of the interior doors, save the single bathroom, had locks. For whatever reason, A.J. felt a sort of protective instinct for the Wells family, and he muscled past Liam to be the first into the room.

"Easy, cowboy!" Liam chided.

A.J. ignored him, gently pushing the door open.

The room stood in complete contrast to the rest of the home, bright and airy and colorful to her dad's dark lair. Mall posters of Duran Duran and Rick Springfield lined the walls next to a concert print of Quarterflash. Magazine photos of Pat Benatar and The Runaways were thumbtacked to the cheap drywall over Jeannie's vanity. A single black and white four-by-six portrait of Eric Somerville was tacked over the other pictures, staring distantly at the photographer.

Liam went to the far side of Jeannie's wrought-iron bed and carefully looked through the sundry "girl" things littering her study desk. "She must have a journal or something—"

"No way, man," A.J. shot back immediately. "We're not snooping in her—" The last words were interrupted as he absently nudged open the nightstand drawer, revealing a locked pink diary. "Shit."

Suddenly Kris called from the kitchen. "Uh, guys?"

The pickup's tires on the gravel drive were already audible, and A.J. bolted from the bedroom. Liam followed, pausing long enough to grab the diary from its drawer and close the bedroom door behind him. He pocketed the pink book in his Army coat and made the back door just as Kris exited.

By the time Mr. Wells had parked the truck and come to the front door, the boys and their bikes had disappeared into the trees.

They skidded to a sideways halt in a forest clearing just north of town, above a small deer path that led down to the main road. The burned-out stumps of old-growth cedar created semi-sheltered structures the local teens used for camp-outs and picnics, or cutting class to pound beers and smoke weed. Liam produced Jeannie's diary from his pocket, and A.J.'s eyes widened in utter disbelief.

"What the hell—?"

He was silenced by the appearance of the Swiss Army knife in Liam's other hand. A.J. wasn't so much surprised. Liam was precisely the kind of kid who packed a Swiss Army knife, and other tools and weapons, in various pockets on his person. He was more apprehensive at how the bigger kid, the bully of bullies, intended to use it.

He set the diary on his bike seat, flipped the small blade open and fished the toothpick from the utility knife's red metal housing, and within a minute had picked the tiny lock holding the book closed.

A.J. and Kris closed around Liam slowly, their curiosity trumping their nervousness.

To his credit, Liam opened the diary at the end and scanned backward, clearly looking only for clues to Jeannie's possible whereabouts. A.J. felt a familiar sense of proprietary jealousy as Liam flipped the pages back one by one.

"Come on, man," he scowled, kicking a foot into the dusty floor of the clearcut. "What does it say?"

Liam flipped another page, working his way backward in time. "Well, her home life is more fucked up than we thought. Pop's drinking himself to death, and she's having trouble dealing with her straight-A, squeaky-clean image."

Kris stared at Liam like he would a riveting TV show. A.J. frowned and dug his hands into his hoodie's kangaroo pocket. "Shit."

"She knows Eric's planning on leaving after he graduates...seems torn between wanting to take off with him and staying here to help her dad."

Liam did his best to keep his report clinical and avoid any salacious interpretation of Jeannie's innermost feelings poured out on paper. "As I thought. They were parking at the Bluff. Like, a lot."

"Close it up," A.J. ordered. "Let's go to the Bluff."

"What else?" Kris asked innocently.

A.J. wasn't having the delay. "What do you mean, 'What else'? They went to the Bluff to park. Close it up! We should be looking for clues there!"

"I think he means, 'What else did they do up there?'," Liam winked at Kris. "You did take sex ed, right?"

"Come on guys!" A.J. went back to his bike and threw his leg over the frame to straddle it.

Kris blinked. A filmy sweat broke out on his forehead.

Liam leaned over to him, lowering his voice to a near whisper. "They've been doing the dirty," he said, making a circle with the fingers of his left hand and penetrating it repeatedly with his right index finger.

A.J. pretended not to hear, pedaling out of the clearing in a huff. Liam replaced the knife and the diary in their respective pockets and picked up the Frankenbike from the ground. He was away almost immediately.

Kris ran to his bike and followed Liam out of the clearing, trying to lose the red flush from his nose and cheeks.

Track 3:
MOVE IN LIGHT
Modern English (1981)

It was a short half-mile to North Bank road, then the better part of a ten-minute ride east along the river to Indian Bluff. Late afternoon birdsong and the smell of fish and pine assaulted their senses, eyes watering as they pedaled against the river. As they approached the turnout, their presence was noticed by Deputy Pete Halverson, his thick face with close-set brown eyes glowering from beneath the flat brim of his "Smokey Bear" hat.

Halverson was just 28, but he'd grown up in Calico, been a high school football star, was injured in a game, and never left town. Although the county seat was five miles away in Gold Beach, Pete still lived in the family home in Calico. He'd opted to remain a big fish in a small pond instead of exercising an ounce of ambition.

The deputy's brown patrol Bronco was parked at an angle on the bluff, nose pointing across the clearcut toward Old Town. The emergency light bar atop the vehicle flashed red and blue, though the engine was shut off, and the gold Curry County insignia shone in stark contrast to the white door panel. Halverson stepped forward and held up a hand, signaling the boys to halt.

As A.J. braked to a stop on the turnout, he noticed Halverson was standing next to a strange marking on the ground. Kris pulled up next to him and noticed it too—the shape looked like it had been burned into the very rock at their feet. It appeared to be a triangular glyph a meter across, with a circular point in the middle, and sections of each side cut away so that only the corners were visible. A.J. immediately thought of the town scare back in 1972, blamed on a Satanic cult that supposedly lived in the Rogue River-Siskiyou National Forest. Two teens had disappeared from the Bluff and never returned. Some folks thought they'd just left town. Others, like A.J., remained convinced it was the cult, and that they were still out there in the deep woods of Oregon, sacrificing babies and eating s'mores with the Dark Lord.

Liam slowed and hung at the back of the group.

"Hold up! Hold up!" Halverson ordered with a level of official bluster that would have been hilarious if it weren't so sad.

"What's...uh, what's going on, Deputy Halverson?" A.J. inquired.

"Hey, Pete," quipped Liam from the back of the group. The subtle disrespect of a tin badge had the desired effect of a glare from Halverson.

"Jennings," Halverson pointed at A.J., "you're tight with the Wells family. Any idea where Jeannie or her boyfriend might have gone?"

A.J. swallowed hard. "Uh, no...I don't actually...I'm not that close..."

"Pete? Who's up there?" cried a voice from below the lip of the bluff. The three boys pushed their bikes forward, still astride, peering over the edge of the turnout. The road's edge was without a guard rail, and fell away a good fifty feet to the floor of the clearcut below. Sitting nose-down at the bottom of the steep grade was Eric Somerville's 1974 Chevy Nova, midnight green save for splotches of primer gray. The windows were up, doors shut, emergency brake likely set. The car was undamaged, which was a head-scratcher, given it looked like it had gone off the bluff and slid down the hill.

Standing next to the Nova, just paces away from her own Bronco with flashing lights, was Sheriff Linda Chavez. She was what folks called "compact". A solid 150 pounds of muscle in a petite five-foot-two frame, Chavez looked like she could take Halverson in an arm-wrestling match, and probably had. Her shoulder-length, raven curls were pulled back in a low bun under her hat, and her shirt cuffs were rolled up to her elbows, exposing well-tanned arms—unusual in a region of pale people who liked to joke, "Oregonians don't tan, they rust." She was proud of her Latina ethnicity, and of being the first woman to hold the elected post, after the previous Sheriff of Curry County was forced to resign amid numerous sex abuse scandals and a rather large wrongful death lawsuit. "What are you kids doing out here?"

A.J. liked Sheriff Chavez. He waved slightly and managed a smile. "Hi Sheriff. We were, um, just riding. Kris found a fishing spot up by Lobster Creek Bridge." He immediately regretted the statement, as the three carried precisely zero fishing equipment, and he was sure Deputy Halverson would take notice of that.

To everyone's surprise, Pete kept his attention on the glyph, snapping a shot with a Polaroid camera and tossing it through the

Bronco's open window onto the dashboard to develop.

Chavez squinted from below the group of boys in the turnout. "You're not headed into Old Town, are you?"

"What? Um, no. It's off limits." A.J. answered dutifully.

"Correct," replied the Sheriff. "Don't forget that. Alright, *vámonos*."

Halverson began waving them away immediately. "Let's go. Clear out, boys."

Chavez returned to her investigation of the Nova, and the three teens returned to the main road.

They rode on, equal parts shaken and exhilarated by the encounter with Curry County's finest. Kris pedaled hard to center himself in the pack.

"Did you see that...what was it? A shape, I guess?"

A.J. nodded. "It seemed familiar to me."

Liam was more sanguine. "This is worse than I thought," he scowled. "Eric loves that car. There's no way he would have just left it there. And did you notice the damage?"

"What damage?" Kris frowned, trying to remember.

"Exactly," Liam said. "There wasn't any. How does a Super Sport with the weight of a three-fifty V-8 under the hood roll down a fifty-foot grade and just stop? It should've rolled out into the clearcut at least. But I didn't even see a ding on that front-end."

"Parking brake?" A.J. mused.

Liam shook his head, standing up on his pedals to coast. "Not buying it. The whole thing smells. It smells like piss."

"So whether they left or were taken by force," Kris began thoughtfully, "where is the most likely place to go?"

"To hide," Liam asked, "or to be hidden?"

"Either one."

A.J. stood and pumped his pedals. "Old Town," he said, angling east onto the old dirt access road.

Kris and Liam followed, pedaling silently for the remainder of the journey, pulling off the main road and onto an old dirt path made by wooden wagons a century ago.

As the calendar neared summer, southern Oregon had the virtue of later sunsets; the afternoons and evenings seemed suspended in an endless golden stasis. A.J. knew they wouldn't completely lose light until 8:49 p.m., and he had until then to check in with his parents. That left them with a solid couple of hours to search before even considering the trip back. The boys rode with purpose, the only sound the rotation of greased bicycle chain driving gear sprockets and the occasional thump of a lose rock kicked aside by a knobby front tire. With the late sun at their backs, they turned with the wheel ruts to make their final approach from the south.

A massive, professionally-painted wooden sign greeted their arrival, warning of the *HAZARDOUS AREA* beyond, and the potential criminal and legal ramifications of proceeding past that point. It bore the full authority of the Curry County Sheriff's Department, and the boys pedaled by, indifferent to its urged caution.

Old Town Calico resembled an abandoned western movie set, down to the scrub brush poking up from packed, dry dirt, and old buildings on the verge of collapse. It had been a typical boomtown with a single main street, on either side of which had stood a line of timber frame buildings. All the necessities of Old West life had once been here: the hotel, saloon, sheriff's office, and livery, with the bank strategically placed at the north end of the strip near the mine entrance. Once-proud facades sagged, weathered and rotten, with many of the buildings having collapsed or been damaged by the sinkholes that accompanied the mine explosions and toxic gas cloud that followed.

Liam was first off his bike, ditching the monstrosity behind an old wooden outhouse that remained mostly upright at the southeast corner of the main street. The small structure had been a satellite of the saloon, which stood deceptively intact just a few yards to the north. Wielding his treasured Maglite 6-D like a weapon, he approached the sagging door of the outhouse.

"Lucy, I'm home!" he chirped, hooking the door with the toe of his Army boot and flinging it open.

He disappeared inside as A.J. and Kris dumped their bikes next to Liam's, taking stock of their surroundings. Several of the more precarious buildings, including the saloon nearby, were adorned with warning placards from the Sheriff's Department, advertising how unsafe the location was and what the legal consequences of trespassing were. Not that Curry County actually had the manpower to enforce such warnings, which was why exploring Old Town was a rite of passage.

Kris and A.J. stepped out into the street, sun low on their left. Liam had just emerged triumphantly from the outhouse with a century-old horseshoe nail when they heard it: a faint, feminine cry for help.

Each boy shivered in succession as they ran through the possible sources for such a sound, finally returning to reality. The cry was of human origin, and it was coming from inside the saloon.

Liam pocketed the nail and turned his flashlight toward the saloon doorway. The exterior doors had fallen off long ago, and the doorway itself was skewed at a precarious angle like a funhouse ride. The three boys entered the darkened, dusty interior, padding quietly with all senses on high alert. Tables and chairs had been left in place, now broken and scattered around the outer orbit of the establishment. The bar itself had broken in the middle, caved into a V shape, the long horizontal mirror behind it shattered and mildew-spotted. The center of the saloon floor had collapsed into one of the many sinkholes that swallowed Old Town, broken planks of oak thrust upward in a conical spiral.

The beam from Liam's Maglite roamed across the sundered floorboards, down into the pit that fell almost ten feet below. As it hit the pale shape of a human hand, the same cry wafted up from the pit in the floor, and A.J. knew they'd found her.

Jeannie Wells, barefoot and clad in torn blue jeans and a zippered hoodie, lay at the bottom of the saloon sinkhole. Her face was ashen and her hair stringy and matted with sweat. A.J. noted the same glyph from Indian Bluff seemed to be tattooed—or rather, *branded*—into the flesh of her inner left wrist.

"Help, please!" came the exhausted plea. "Someone?"

A.J. went to the edge of the pit and leveled his gaze at the shivering girl. He knew it was her before she came into view. "Jeannie? Hang on, we got ya..."

Constructing a bosun's chair from the nylon rope he always carried on his bike, Liam and A.J. hauled Jeannie from the sinkhole, while Kris rode back to the Bluff and notified Sheriff Chavez and Deputy Halverson about their discovery. Though almost catatonic, Jeannie recognized A.J. and grabbed him in a desperate hug once out of the pit and on her feet.

"Oh my God," she repeated in a guttural whisper. "Oh my God, oh my God."

Flooded with questions and fear alike, A.J. and Liam guided the girl from the death trap interior of the saloon to the dusty main street outside. A.J. asked about her experiences as delicately as possible, but Jeannie only repeated her mantra: "Oh my God, oh my

God." The boys ultimately gave up any attempt at questioning, and walked her with their bikes to the sign at the south end of Old Town.

They crossed their fingers that Chavez would take the net gain of rescuing Jeannie and not prosecute them for trespassing in Old Town. Since their story of hearing Jeannie's call for help as they were riding past Old Town on the way to their fishing spot was somewhat if not entirely plausible, the gamble made sense—and to a large degree it worked. Turned loose with a warning and a reluctant thank you, the boys and their bikes were transported back to town in Halverson's Bronco while Sheriff Chavez took Jeannie to the medical center in Gold Beach.

Halverson dropped the boys off at the diner, just before he was called away to a car fire on the Wedderburn Bridge section of Highway 101. All three friends were buzzing with adrenaline and excitement, and none of them knew how far from over the evening actually was.

Track 4:
LET'S WORK
Prince (1981)

The dinner rush on Fridays usually manifested in a packed dining room, with the single old-timers hunched over the bar, and families celebrating payday in the double line of booths opposite. Kris' mom ran the front-of-house, while his dad supervised the kitchen staff, one part head chef, one part orchestra conductor. But the only music audible was the crackle of a 45 RPM record on the 1970 Rock-Ola jukebox: The Cars' single *Since You're Gone*, pulsing and retching like a sick cat from its bassy, blown-out cabinet speakers.

Kris donned his cap and apron and went to work, while A.J. and Liam scooted into a booth. Burgers and Cokes came out automatically, and at the family discount, which most often meant "free".

A.J. caught the milky eye of Kristof's grandmother behind the counter as she rolled out and filled a new batch of *pierogi*, offering a toast with his glass of Coke. She stared at him a moment and then returned to her work, leaving A.J. uncomfortable and a bit befuddled. He returned his attention to Liam and was about to mention possible origins for the glyph they'd seen, but the older boy was transfixed on something in the distance. A.J. turned to glance over his shoulder and saw the object of Liam's attention.

Molly leaned into the *Asteroids* machine and pounded away on the fire button, pulverizing wire-frame obstacles into space dust. A new arrival to Calico, she was thirteen and just about to move into eighth grade in September. A pair of padded headphones encircled her neck, almost lost in the oversized hood of an orchid-colored pullover sweatshirt. The cord ran down her front to the Sony Walkman clipped to the waistband of her jeans. Her auburn hair was long on top, shaved on the back and sides, its length pulled back in a ponytail that displayed the buzzed under-portion and the multiple piercings in her ears. Her complexion was smooth and as tan as one would expect an outdoor kid from California to be, with a small constellation of freckles stippled across her nose and cheeks. She was small and lithe, and shifted her weight back and forth on white leather Converse trainers.

When the two boys had finished their meals and bused their own plates to the wash tub behind the bar, Liam went to put a quarter on the *Asteroids* game in direct challenge to Molly, who had, in a short half hour, knocked his high score down to number two.

A.J. went into the back kitchen to confab with Kris and his grandmother. With Kris translating back and forth from English to Polish, A.J. showed a drawing of the strange glyph they'd seen at the Bluff and branded into Jeannie's wrist.

"Ask her if she's ever seen a symbol like this," A.J. instructed. Kris pointed at the drawing and asked his grandmother, who simply peered at the two boys through her white eye and shook her head.

"*Nie*," was her soft reply.

A.J. was disappointed. The old lady was usually a font of Old World knowledge and trivia. She had at least a dozen ways of warding off the Evil Eye, and could predict the weather more accurately than the Farmer's Almanac.

Kris shrugged. "Sorry, dude." Then he blinked and remembered the 24-volume set of Time-Life Books he and his dad had found at a garage sale in Medford a few years ago. They were illustrated with all sorts of harrowing paintings of supernatural themes, which had scared Kris out of his wits when he was nine. "Oh, wait!" he blurted, snapping his fingers. "We have that set of *Man, Myth & Magic* back at the house!" He immediately regretted doing so, as it effectively blocked any hope of the guys hanging out at the diner for videogames and free cola. Now he'd be under pressure to leave work early and go wherever adventure led them.

Fortunately his mother, a Reubenesque woman with gray streaks in her pinned-up auburn hair, took note of the dining room— now largely vacant—and told Kris to hang up his apron for the night. A.J. made small talk with Mrs. Korolewski while his friend went to clean up, and got her permission for Kris to spend the night at his place for an epic *D&D* campaign they were supposedly finishing up.

Kris grabbed his jacket off a wall peg in the back, nodding toward the front door, where Liam and the "new girl" stood chatting. Molly looked decidedly unimpressed with Liam's tales of having built a set of nunchucks in shop class.

A.J. peered over his glasses as the four gathered by the door. "Who's this?" he asked.

Molly squinted at him. "*This* is Molly," she shot back.

"Her family bought the old Chambers place up on the hill," Liam explained. "They're real estate developers. Her brother was an all-state quarterback back in California."

A.J. flashed a look of disbelief at Liam. "Jesus, dude. What's her favorite color?"

"Purple," Molly smirked. "Your buddy here was saying you've been out at Old Town and found that missing girl, Jeannie?"

Kris flushed red and shoved his hands into the pockets of his jeans. "Yeah, that was us."

"Cool." Molly looked impressed for the first time since she'd entered the diner. "So what are you up to now?"

"We're going to look up a symbol we saw at the Bluff in my books and then we're going back out to Old Town," Kris blurted. "Wanna come?"

The idea of a girl tagging along on their expedition didn't sit well with A.J., though he wasn't sure why. Molly seemed okay, and Liam was sure doing his best to vouch for her while Kris blushed his way through the conversation. It was clear the two of them had no problem including her.

"Hold up," A.J. warned. "We haven't actually planned anything."

But before he knew what was happening, they were outside, heading around the back of the restaurant to the rustic home Kris shared with his parents and grandmother. Once in Kris' bedroom, with books spread out on the dingy, rust-colored carpet, A.J. found his focus. He and Kris poured over the sections on angelic and alien symbols, while Molly looked at the volume on ESP and Liam rocked out to the mix tape in Molly's Walkman.

The music he heard was a revelation. A kid from rural Oregon with access to only a couple of classic rock stations and a country station, Liam had been raised on a steady diet of bands referred to by single-word names: Zeppelin, Stones, Skynyrd, and bands that only had single words in their names to begin with: Styx, Rush, Kiss. Occasionally Mr. Korolewski would bring back a 45 from Portland for the diner's juke box—The Cars, Pretenders or Quarterflash: something popular on that new MTV cable network—not that Calico had cable at all.

But Molly's mix tape was a banquet of punk, post-punk, and new romantic alternative rock that Liam could never have imagined existing. Siouxsie and the Banshees. Bauhaus. The Clash. Joy Division. Japan. This was high culture that kids from Los Angeles brought with them to the northern wilds as a gift to the natives. He was just hitting the opening drum cadence of Black Flag's *Gimme Gimme Gimme* when A.J. announced he'd found their mysterious icon in a section on alien languages.

Liam removed the thin pair of headphones, immediately realizing how loud he'd had the volume. "You found it?"

A.J. turned the book so the others could see it, producing his sketch of the symbol for comparison. "Doesn't say anything about what it means," he qualified, "just that it's been found at UFO crash sites and stuff." He was quite disappointed that its origin wasn't among the arcane scripts among the books. Surely that was more appropriate for Satanists.

Kris let out a low whistle and Molly chuckled nervously.

"Creeeeeepy," she said musically.

A.J. glanced at the alarm clock on Kris' nightstand. "Okay," he said, "it's almost nine. How's everyone for curfew?"

Liam grinned ear-to-ear. "Dude. *School's out!*"

Kris got the Alice Cooper reference and joined Liam singing incorrectly, "*...for the weekend!*"

Molly rolled her eyes in the way only a thirteen-year-old girl can do. "My folks are in

Grant's Pass for a sales seminar. They left my brother in charge. *Technically*."

"What does *technically* mean?" asked A.J.

"It means I can call him and say I'm spending the night at Allison's house, and he'll be fine with it."

A.J. thumbed through his mental Rolodex for any Allisons he might know. None sprang to mind. "Who's Allison?" he asked.

Molly shrugged, giving A.J. a half-smile that made him suddenly feel warm in his chest.

They took turns making calls to parents, the boys spinning the tale of the *D&D* game at A.J.'s, except for A.J., who said the game was at Liam's. Molly called her older brother, Bodhi, about spending the night at Allison's and being home before too late Saturday afternoon. That was just fine with Bodhi, who apparently had a girl over anyway.

And with the alibis set and the plan in place, A.J., Kris, Liam, and Molly headed out on their bikes into the dark streets of Calico, Oregon.

Track 5:
GHOST TOWN
The Specials (1981)

With battery-powered headlamps, they pedaled into the night, stopping first at Liam's garage, where the boys loaded their backpacks with miscellaneous gear: flashlights, road flares, a pair of Radio Shack walkie-talkies, and a hundred feet of coiled nylon climbing rope, which Molly ended up slinging across her shoulder like a bandoleer. Liam also insisted on bringing a ten-foot length of one-inch PVC pipe in reference to the standard tool taken by all of his *D&D* characters on their adventures. It had started as a ten-foot length, but was now actually only eight-foot-four, as Liam's mom had cut as needed to fix the bathroom sink. Liam carried it under his arm like a jousting lance.

Molly had put her brother's latest mix tape into her Walkman, and had the volume set loud. Bodhi had the habit of naming his mixes after obscure literary references, and this one was called *I Sing the Body Electric*, after the Ray Bradbury short story. It consisted largely of guitar-based rock and new wave like Elvis Costello, The Vapors, and The Pretenders. As the Calico kids zoomed off toward Indian Bluff and beyond, Chrissy Hynde's vocal refrain from *Mystery Achievement* swam in Molly's ears. She felt almost as if Chrissy was speaking to her, on a primal, nostalgic, *Scooby Doo* level.

They cut off the access road as before, approaching Old Town from the southern curve. The moon sat obscured by a diffusion of high clouds, bathing the ruins of old Calico in a dim light. Rickety facades of the buildings lining Main Street poked up in silhouette, disappearing in the distance toward the mines.

The four dropped their bikes in front of the saloon where the three boys had found Jeannie, and decided after some cajoling, daring, and counter-daring to explore the hotel across the street. The structure was at this point little more than a hollow box, its wooden walls and floors rotten and creaking in the breeze. A.J. warned that it might collapse at any time and was too dangerous to investigate at night. But Liam prevailed, citing the allegedly massive size of his testicles as reasoning. Molly rolled her eyes, but volunteered to go with him anyway. The two of them disappeared inside, accompanied by Liam's PVC pipe.

Kris and A.J. decided that discretion, and not getting tetanus, was the better part of valor, and said they'd keep watch outside.

As Liam and Molly worked their way around the inside walls toward the old staircase, Liam used the plastic pole to tap and jab at various tears and ridges in the buckled floorboards. The hotel interior was dark and musty, filled with shudders and groans and the occasional jump scare when a rat crossed the beam of Molly's flashlight.

Aside from a century's worth of dust and holes in the floor where the boards had rotted and fallen in, the main level was devoid of anything interesting. The hotel had been one of the last structures to be abandoned when the town packed up to move, and had been thoroughly cleared out. Anything of value or historical significance had been looted by curious and adventuresome teens or souvenir hunters over the intervening years.

"Nothing much down here," Liam muttered.

Molly shined her flashlight across the lower half of the staircase to the second floor. "Stairs look okay."

Liam swallowed hard. "Um, yeah...sure."

A.J. peered in through one of the empty window frames. "Aww, hell," he sighed. "They're gonna go upstairs." He turned back to Kris, who was frozen in a terrified tableau, eyes wide and fixed on the north end of Main Street.

At first Kris had thought it was the reflection of a car headlight, but as it moved, he began to pick out some detail. It was of a graceful, generally feminine shape, glowing a bright phosphorescent white at the center, and gradually diffusing to an invisible edge. It floated slowly, ethereally, from the corner of the old hardware store, on a diagonal path across Main Street to the collapsed warehouse on the opposite side.

It checked all of the boxes for being a ghost, and Kris stood petrified on the rotting hotel porch, knees locked in absolute fear.

A.J. stared at his friend in surprise. "Kris? Hey, what's up, buddy?"

Kris didn't answer, but A.J. could see beads of sweat beginning to form on his brow. Taking a cue from where his friend's eyes were focused, he quickly glanced the same direction, but saw nothing. The apparition had vanished.

"Did...did you see it?" Kris stammered.

"See what?"

"I...dunno. Looked like a..."

"Like a what?"

Kris began to unlock his muscles as the sense of threat faded and his fight-or-flight response subsided in kind. "Nothing," he said quietly.

Inside the hotel, Molly led Liam up the age-worn staircase, still standing due to its oak construction alone. Nonetheless, eight steps from the top landing, Molly put her foot in precisely the wrong spot, and punched a hole in a stair tread.

She fell forward with a grunt. "Ugh. Shit."

"You okay?" Liam was immediately two stairs above, turning back to offer her assistance. "Here, grab my pole," he smirked.

Molly again rolled her eyes. "Jesus," she sighed. "How long have you been waiting to make that joke?"

She took hold of the PVC pipe regardless, and Liam anchored them as she removed her leg from the sundered stair and hopped lightly up to the top landing.

"Long enough, apparently," Liam grinned.

The hotel had eight guest rooms on the second floor, four on each side of the gallery. Unfortunately the floor itself had caved in over the western corner of the structure, leaving that wing inaccessible. Molly and Liam were restricted to the eastern wing, in whose hallway they stood on creaky floorboards.

Taking great care with every step, the two tiptoed to the farthest room, noticing its door had come off the top hinge, and was sitting open at a cocked angle. Molly, being small and fearless, squeezed past the crooked door and flashed her light around the room. A century-old wrought iron bed frame rusted in the corner, next to a pile of wood and glass debris that had probably been a nightstand and oil lamp at some point. The space was otherwise empty.

Molly ducked back into the gallery hall. "Nothing," she said, directing her light toward the second room, which was minus a door altogether.

They entered the second room, flashlights revealing a space almost identical to the first, but without the bed frame and debris. Liam could tell Molly was getting antsy, but didn't want to be the first to chicken out.

"There's nothing here," she said. "I'm gonna check the third one."

Then she was gone, and Liam stood alone in a dusty room, in a creaky hotel, in an Oregon ghost town. A shiver ran down his spine and he turned to follow, but stopped when the beam from his flashlight hit something shiny on the floor by the doorway. He leaned the plastic pole against the corner of the room and bent down, brushing some dust and wear from a large coin, turning it over in his hand.

It was slightly tarnished silver, with an eagle on one side, and a seated woman holding a shield that said LIBERTY on the other. The date stamp was 1870.

Excited beyond words, Liam pocketed the coin and grabbed his PVC pole from the corner. He stepped back out into the hall as Molly put her foot through a rotten floorboard and fell forward again.

"Ugh. Goddamn it!" she huffed.

Again, Liam was at her side, offering assistance.

"Here, take—"

"Yeah, yeah, give me your pole."

Liam braced himself and hauled Molly from the hole in the floor. She was not amused.

"You've never dated, have you?" she inquired.

"Sure I have. Lots of times," he said. As he spoke, Liam's cheek twitched, signaling Molly that he was lying.

"Uh huh," Molly sighed at an Olympic level of proficiency. "Let's check the last room and get out of here."

As they turned toward the last guest room, door missing like the second, a hissed shout echoed from downstairs.

"Hey! Guys! Get down here!"

Liam and Molly made eye contact for a moment, and without saying a word, headed for the stairwell. Treading delicately down the stairs while avoiding the pits and holes beneath was like skiing the world's slowest downhill slalom.

They exited the hotel onto the sagging porch, Liam thrilled to share the news of his find.

"Hey, guess what I found upstairs..."

Molly cut him off with a slap to the arm, nodding at A.J. and Kris, who were frozen in place, eyes locked on the north end of town. Multiple apparitions floated from a vanishing point in the distance, dispersing into town among the rotting structures and ruins of Old Calico.

A.J. pointed. "Is that what you saw before?"

Kris nodded in the affirmative. "Just one, though."

Liam had questions. "Wait. Before? When did you...what are...Jesus, look how many!"

"I count about a dozen," Molly said, switching off her flashlight and stepping silently from the hotel porch.

"Wait, Molly!" A.J. hissed. "Where are you going?"

"I wanna get closer," was the whispered reply, then she disappeared into the shadows of the ruins along Main Street.

A.J. awoke from his reverie, whether out of a sense of obligation to protect the new girl from whatever was flitting from the mines, or a sense of self-preservation lest anything happen to Molly that would be awkward to explain to parents and authorities. "Come on," he instructed. "Try to keep to the shadows." Then he was off as well.

Liam and Kris followed, not to be outdone by a "chick and a nerd", taking off in a stooped run straight from a bad WWII movie. Liam muttered, "Serpentine," as he zigged and zagged toward the livery stable.

Molly peered around the corner of the stable and felt a cold hand on the back of her neck. Spinning instantly, her left arm shot out and knocked A.J.'s flashlight to the ground. "Sheeeit!" she hissed through clenched teeth. "Don't do that!"

"Sorry," A.J. protested. "I couldn't see where you'd stopped." He tried to look past her toward Main Street, but the silhouette of her head blocked his view. Her hair smelled like strawberry Suave.

A sudden burst of light erupted from the night sky, like a photographer's strobe. All four of the teens cast their eyes skyward, as if to check the weather for an impending storm, but it was the same moon slung high behind the same scattered clouds. What had changed?

Molly was first to notice. "Hey," she whispered, gesturing down Main Street toward the mine entrance in the distance. "They're gone."

The boys stepped gingerly away from the corner of the stable and verified that, yes, the apparitions, which had populated the old ghost town just moments ago, had vanished. The ruins of Old Town sat as still and silent as ever.

"What now?" A.J. asked, clearly shaken by the sudden, eerie quiet.

Liam flicked on his flashlight and stepped into the dusty street. "I'm gonna check out the mine." He knew only the bravest of older high school kids ever ventured anywhere near the mine opening. If the rest of Old Town was hazardous due to the sinkholes and century-old buildings which threatened to collapse at any moment, the mine was exponentially so. No excuse was good enough to spin at Sheriff Chavez that would avoid the most epic grounding by his mom if anything happened in there. Liam was therefore certain it would impress Molly. He took a deep breath and prepared his legs to carry him to the end of Main Street and up the incline to the mouth of the tunnel. A.J. made a frustrated motion to make him stop. Molly rolled her eyes so hard it gave her a headache.

"HOLY SHIT!"

Everyone jumped, turning toward Kris, who stood frozen to the ground, absolutely petrified, gaping at something at the far end of his flashlight beam. Something on the other side of the livery window. As the others crowded around their friend to take in his view, their mouths each fell open in amazement.

A slender, pale face, long-haired and sunken-eyed, stared back at them. Although lean, the jaw was square, the brow furrowed in a look of rudderless shock. Instantly, the boys knew exactly who it was.

Track 6:
NOTHING TO FEAR
(BUT FEAR ITSELF)
Oingo Boingo (1981)

E ric Somerville.
He was alive—or at least appeared so—albeit slightly the worse for wear. But he was solid and real, unlike the apparitions they'd just seen. A.J. scrambled to the stable door, which had been reduced to a barricade of cracked and moldy planks that leaned criss-crossed against the sides of the opening. The roof had mostly fallen in over time, and the structure was unstable enough that nobody wanted to leave Eric stuck inside.

The others followed A.J., pitching in to re-move enough of the broken planks to create an opening wide enough for him to get through.

Pushing his glasses high onto his nose and aiming his flashlight into the dark interior, A.J. stepped into the old livery stable. Broken crates and a few rusted barrel hoops were the only contents, save Eric himself. The boy was a strapping six-footer, with shoulder-length chestnut hair. He was clad in well-worn blue jeans, his feet and upper torso bare. Turning in the beam of the flashlight, his mouth opened and he tried to speak, but no sound emerged.

A.J. approached cautiously. "Eric?" he croaked. "Hey, man..." As he slowly padded toward the boy, he happened to glance down, and noticed the same strange glyph that they'd all seen up at Indian Bluff, burned into the dirt floor. A.J. made a point to side-step around it.

As A.J. came toward Eric, he could see the older kid blink, and suddenly turn to look at him.

"Hello?" came the hoarse greeting. "Are you real?"

A.J. suddenly felt his fear turn to sympathy, and his heart sank. "Yeah, man. We got ya. Come with me." He took Eric's arm, looking down to see that the same glyph Jeannie was found branded with, the same glyph that they were finding all over the ground in Old Town and at the Bluff, was likewise branded into his left wrist.

As A.J. slowly guided Eric toward the livery door, carefully keeping away from the shape seared into the dirt, he tried a basic line of questioning. "Do you remember what happened to you?"

Eric's eyes were blank. "No. Where's Jeannie?"

"She's okay, man. We found her."

"She's okay?"

"Yeah, buddy. She's fine."

"I-I need to get home."

A.J. guided him by the arm out to the remaining three, Eric walking tender-footed on the stony ground. Liam shrugged out of his baggy Army jacket and offered it to the older boy, whom it fit much better. Together and in complete silence, the four walked Eric back to the edge of Old Town where their bikes awaited. The question, really, was how to get him home, as they were one bike short. After a bit of petty logistical debate, Molly volunteered to ride on the rear rack of the Kricycle and let Eric use her purple unisex BMX.

They rode back in silence, surrounding Eric to make sure he didn't veer randomly off-course.

When the headlights hit them, A.J. was convinced it was another brilliant flash signifying one of them was about to disappear. One by one, each kid skidded to a halt at the outside of the curve, shielding their eyes from the glare of halogen headlamps. A black 1980 Ford Fairmont sedan sat idling in the middle of the road, between them and Perry's Bridge, a structure straddling one of the many tributaries of the Rogue River. The first of the old timber access paths stretched off the main road just a few dozen yards beyond, but they'd have to cross the bridge to get there.

Kris was already sweating from the ride, but his exertion had become panic. "Who is that?"

A.J. had heard stories about government agents in black cars showing up during UFO investigations, threatening individuals, or making them "disappear". He had no desire for such an encounter. "No one we want to meet," was his answer.

"They're blocking the bridge," Liam observed.

"Really?" Molly sighed. "Hadn't noticed."

The black car revved its engine from a hundred yards away, tires screaming on the old asphalt road. With a steep, wooded hillside to the right, the river to the left, and a menacing vehicle blocking their access to the back road into town, there was only one option.

"Follow me!" A.J. shouted, spinning his bike on its rear tire and pedaling hard the way they'd just come. The others followed suit, try-

ing to keep up—Kris pumping his legs furious-
ly with the extra body to carry.

The car roared up the road, painting their
backs in white light, pulling closer with each
second.

They rounded the turn and were hitting
the crest of a rise near a turnout when A.J.
suddenly pulled off the road and stood in the
saddle, walking on his bike pedals as he nosed
up the hillside, thick with trees. Eric followed,
then Liam. Kris' bike struggled under the awk-
wardness of two riders, and he skidded, almost ditching the bike along with Molly. Gripping one wrist with her other hand, arms encircling his waist, she held on for dear life,
sneakered feet sticking to the pegs on the rear
wheel. He recovered with a subtle adjustment
to the front fork, and followed the others in
doubling back.

The Ford flew past them, losing track of
the riders in the woods. It skidded into a 180-
degree turn, fishtailing as the engine revved
again.

Without wasting a moment, A.J. steered
down the hillside and onto the road in their
original direction. The black Ford closed the
distance in seconds, engine snarling as they
flew toward the bridge.

This would be dicey.

If the car so much as clipped one of them, there was nothing to stop them from wiping out on the rocks and freezing water. There was no way to avoid the vehicle on a small timber bridge that was only one car wide to begin with. A collective surge of adrenaline hit the group and bike pedals churned faster. They hit the bridge at top speed, knowing there was only one way to go: forward.

Knobby tires vibrated across timber beams, and the car was on them, its front bumper almost knocking the Kricycle. Molly turned momentarily behind to look and was blinded by the headlights. Burying her face in Kris' sweaty back might have been a questionable thought mere minutes ago, but now it was the only semblance of safety in a moment of potential oblivion.

The Ford's engine roared.

Then they were across to the far side, and A.J. led them up onto the timber access trail. The car squealed its tires and tried to turn, then recovered and gunned its engine up toward the access. With brights still glaring, it nosed its grill into the woods, probing the trail slowly. The large sedan was not as agile on the soft, uneven ground—the bikes were much faster and more maneuverable in this environment. A.J. and Eric broke off down a trail to the left. Liam, Kris, and Molly to the right.

Within a few minutes, the sound of the Ford's engine grew distant as the car ceased pursuit and backed out of the timber access road.

Before long, the kids had reunited on the outskirts of town. When they got within sight of the Somerville house, A.J. had a sudden thought.

"Hey, Eric, when you tell your folks about us finding you, maybe don't mention Old Town, huh? We weren't exactly supposed to be out there."

Eric braked to a halt and dismounted the borrowed bicycle, offering it back to Molly. "Sure, man," Eric acknowledged, more lucid than A.J. had seen him that night. Maybe the hard ride while being chased by the mystery car had put his brain back on track. "You found me in a ditch off the main road. That's all I remember."

As Molly accepted her bike back and swung her leg across the frame, Eric winked at her. Ordinarily she might have found it un-warranted and creepy, but in this instance, it was more like a secret code between people who had endured a crisis together.

"Chavez would give you guys hell," he said blankly, although A.J. could have sworn the corner of his right lip curled up almost enough to be considered a smirk. Then any indication of levity vanished as he added, "Not to mention whoever was in that black Ford."

"Thanks, man," A.J. said, and the others echoed in kind. "Too bad we didn't have your Nova."

Liam nodded in agreement. "Yeah, that sweet machine would've blown the doors off that Fairmont."

Eric allowed himself a quiet chuckle. "Damn straight."

As the four friends aimed their bikes back into Calico, Eric raised his hand in an awkward wave. "Thank you," he said solemnly, turning toward the porch light of his parents' home as the kids rode away toward town.

"What's the plan?" Molly asked after several moments. "My brother thinks I'm at Allison's tonight."

"We still don't know what's up with those glyphs," A.J. said.

Kris yawned. "And we're not gonna figure it out tonight."

"Anyone up for some *D&D*?" Liam suggested. "I can run my *Death Island* adventure."

"I hate that scenario," Kris complained. "It's always a T-P-K."

Molly frowned. "What's 'T-P-K'?"

"Total Party Kill," A.J. explained, not surprised that her response was a simple shrug. "Anyway, I'm tired."

They turned off North Bank Rogue River Road onto First Avenue, flying past the Calico Saloon, 1st Avenue Grill, and the auto shop. Traffic was almost nonexistent, and they wove and swooped down toward Cedar Street, lost in their own individual thoughts. A.J. had pretty much called it, and the others would follow suit. Their adventure was over, at least for now. There would be more research, probably another expedition back into Old Town, and possibly into the mine. But there would be more preparation, more due diligence. And they had to make sure Sheriff Chavez didn't investigate Eric's return in too much detail.

They slowed to a stop as they passed Cedar, and First Avenue began to climb toward Union Street. Pulling to a stop at the corner by the T-shirt shop, just a block south of the diner, they slapped hands and exchanged smiles at a job well done.

"So our overnight plans fell through," A.J. said. "That's all we need to tell our folks."

Liam saluted. "Tomorrow, then?"

"Meet you at the diner," A.J. promised. "Bright and early."

They pedaled off in their separate ways, A.J. backtracking up First Avenue toward home. He stood in the saddle as he pumped up the incline of Lamont Street, breathing hard, heart pounding in his chest.

It had been quite a day.

Cruising across Fourth Avenue, he hit Hillcrest at blinding speed, flashing back on the day's events, and the music that had pulled him out of bed in the first place.

Track 7:
LOST WEEKEND
Wall of Voodoo (1981)

Saturday morning arrived in a salmon-pink sky dotted with puffy clouds, the air crisp and tinged with the scent of mossy earth. Four friends gathered at the Silver City Diner for a quick breakfast before hashing out the plan to explore Old Town and the glyphs again.

Their plans were waylaid with the arrival of a Sheriff's Department truck in the diner parking lot. Sheriff Chavez entered the restaurant, nodding at the small handful of locals who greeted her.

She eyed the group of teens with a practiced suspicion. "Where you kids off to today?" she asked, innocently enough.

Kris opened his mouth to speak, but A.J. stood from the booth and stepped between them. "Dunno," he shrugged. "We were gonna continue our *D&D* campaign, but it's such a nice day..."

Liam coughed, and A.J. realized he was laying it on a bit thick.

"So...um..." he stammered, "we uh...don't know."

Chavez put her thumbs into her gun belt and regarded the four. Molly slouched in the corner of the booth, the tinny sound of loud music audible through the foam headphones covering her ears. Liam sat across from her, coloring an angular design on his jeans with a black Sharpie. Kris sat next to Molly, still wearing the apron from his morning shift. A.J. quietly slinked back into the booth next to Liam.

"And you guys didn't go back out to Old Town again last night?"

The general murmur of denial was indignant enough to sell their innocence without overplaying it. "No!", "Of course not!", and "It's off limits!" joined a chorus of "We're not *that* stupid!"

"Where did you locate Eric Somerville?" she asked.

Kris was up to bat. "You know Perry's Bridge? Just past there, in a ditch off the main road," he explained, convincingly at that.

Chavez sighed. "I spoke to Eric Somerville this morning," she said, watching the kids sweat—even Molly, who could clearly hear the conversation, headphones notwithstanding. "He confirms your story."

As the group collectively exhaled, she added, "Good job."

A.J. caught a subtle tic from Chavez, which he thought might have actually been a secret wink. It was as though the Curry County Sheriff just wanted plausible deniability, and as long as the kids all had their stories straight, she wouldn't get into trouble if they happened to go where they shouldn't have been.

"Well, if you're looking for something to do," Chavez suggested, "the *Curry County Reporter* wants to do a story on Jeannie and Eric, and you four, apparently."

Liam shifted on the squeaky vinyl seat, instantly uncomfortable with the notion of any kind of fame, local or otherwise. By contrast, Kris' eyes were like saucers.

Chavez almost turned to leave, but swiveled on her booted heel and added, "And then there's the reward."

A shocked, half-mumbled buzz erupted from the four.

"Reward?" Kris marveled.

"A thousand bucks for each missing person. That's two thousand, split four ways. Not bad spending money for the summer."

Blank stares flashed from person to person across the booth, testament to the imaginary shopping sprees being conjured in real time.

"Well it really...I uh..." A.J. stammered.

"This being an election year," Chavez sighed, "I'm afraid your uncle will insist on the photo op."

"I mean," Molly pretested, lowering the headphones to encircle her neck, "what if we just decline?"

"Hey, donate it to charity," Chavez demurred. "I don't really care. But Mayor Vaughn will make this happen, even if he has to write the check from his own bank account. I suggest you smile pretty for the camera, then do whatever the heck you want with the money." She shifted her compact, petite frame within the brown and white rural law enforcement uniform and withdrew her thumbs from her belt, clasping her fingers together and cracking them for effect. "So can I trust you to be at the courthouse at noon, or do you want a lift into town?"

By 'town', of course, she meant Gold Beach, where all the big markers of civilization were: the nearest bank, the nearest movie theater, and the nearest videogame arcade. Not to mention the courthouse and jail.

A quick round of nodding affirmed that the group would assemble at the county courthouse in Gold Beach at noon. Seemingly satisfied, Sheriff Linda Chavez nodded a silent farewell and headed out to her utility vehicle in the parking lot, backing away and disappearing onto Union Street.

"Looks like we're *thousand-aires*," Kris chimed. His Christmas list had suddenly become lighter with the knowledge that he'd be able to afford some nice purchases on his own.

"*You* are, maybe," Molly scoffed. It was almost not worth having to explain to her folks, who already gave her a respectable allowance.

A.J. folded his arms. "You're taking your share, Molly. Two thousand is easier to split four ways."

Liam nodded in agreement. "Also it's *hundred-aires*, Kris. Five hundred each."

"My uncle will want to make sure he gets a photo with us on the cover of the *Reporter*," A.J. complained. "Like Chavez said, this is gold for his re-election."

Molly was skeptical of the entire process. "Dude. By the time we're done in Gold Beach, we won't have any time left to go out to the Bluff or Old Town."

Kris weighed the options of being a local hero in the paper with a nice reward in his pocket, or going back to the scene of the crime and risking the wrath of Sheriff Chavez. "Do we really need to go back there?" he asked almost rhetorically, eyes darting between the occupants of the booth.

"Will you weenies relax?" Liam sighed, exasperated. He pointed a finger at A.J. "We're doing the photo op. I ain't turning down no five-hundred-dollar reward, and I'm happy to take yours off your hands if you don't want it." Then he shifted in the booth seat and turned the same finger on Kris. "We're going back to investigate the symbols at the Bluff. You don't wanna come, you can stay here in your diapers and suck your thumb while we're out there getting stuff done."

Kris gaped as if he'd been hosed down with ice water.

Liam turned to look at Molly, who was ready with her own expression that told him *no matter what you say, you're still a dumbass, and you're not in charge.* His tone softened, and he opened his hands. "We still have Sunday."

With bellies full of scrambled eggs and greasy hash browns, the four pedaled out to the North Bank Rogue River Road, and headed west. It was just over five and a half miles to Wedderburn, a tiny unincorporated neighboring community on the north bank of the Rogue. Had they continued straight, North Bank Rogue River Road would have become Wedderburn Loop, which would have taken them up the coast. But their destination was Gold Beach, on the south bank of the river. The small community lay on the far side of the Isaac Lee Patterson Bridge via the Oregon Coast Highway, home to fewer than two thousand permanent residents and an ever-increasing population of seasonal workers and summer tourists. It was a prime location for commercial real estate, on the nexus of a river mouth to the Pacific and US Route 101.

Coasting across the bridge, they cycled deeper into Gold Beach, past the municipal airport, finally locating the Curry County courthouse at Ellensburg and Moore.

A.J.'s Uncle Bill was his mom's older brother. He was also the three-term mayor of Calico, running for his fourth. Forty-eight and graying at the temples, Bill Vaughn had a barrel chest and lanky limbs, giving him the look of a frog on a dissection plate. He had a formidable mustache and an equally formidable closet full of plaid polyester sport coats a decade old. Liam often described him as the love-child of Magnum P.I. and the mayor from *Jaws*.

Bill was in typical frenetic form, fresh from the restroom and compulsively rubbing his nose. He lit up when he saw the group of kids in the courthouse lobby, making A.J. cringe.

"There's my nephew!" the mayor bellowed, gathering A.J. into a massive bear hug.

"Hey Uncle Bill," A.J. sighed after being released.

"I see you brought the whole gang," said Bill, puffing out his chest and resting a pair of sunbaked hands on his hips. "Not sure I know this little lady," he added, nodding at Molly. "And I make it my business to know everyone in Calico!"

"Molly," she said, waving but making no effort at physical contact. The man creeped her out something fierce. But then most men did, except maybe her dad. And Bodhi. And A.J. wasn't *too* bad.

They were ushered into a side office where the human-interest writer and photographer from the *Curry County Reporter* were waiting. Sheriff Chavez joined them, managing to clench every teenage jaw by her presence. A.J. was just certain she knew their story regarding Eric's rescue was bullshit. But they were committed to the ruse, and had to follow through.

The first few shots resembled a police line-up more than a civic commendation, but after some cajoling from the journalist and amped-up encouragement from Mayor Bill, the four kids managed a range of non-scowls to almost-smirks. There hadn't been enough time to have a giant novelty check made, so the newspaper made do with a few snaps of the kids standing with the mayor and sheriff, and a short interview with A.J., who it turned out had the best ability to spin an interesting yarn without spilling too many of the illicit details.

Mayor Bill handed each of them a check for five hundred dollars, drawn on the Umpqua Bank. They were finished before one o'clock, and headed two blocks east to the branch office, where A.J. and Kris already had savings accounts. Molly's mother, a bottle blond with hairsprayed bangs and a gold blazer, had stopped in to cash a check, and did a double-take when she saw the group.

"Molly? Honey, what are you doing here?"

Initially embarrassed, Molly finally indicated the others. "Guys, this is my mom, Janet. Mom, this is Kris, Liam, and um...A.J."

A.J. noticed the name tag on her blazer featured the logo of Reynolds Real Estate.

The boys offered halfhearted waves and pleasantries, and Molly filled Janet in on the adventure of the past twenty-four hours, the rescue of Eric Somerville, and the reward offered them by the mayor and Sheriff's Department. She left out the part where they'd outrun the mysterious black Ford, or the ghosts they'd seen at Old Town. Or that they'd gone to Old Town in the first place.

Janet looked at the check, impressed. "Why then, my dear," she grinned, "it's time you got an account of your own!"

By the time they were done at the bank, it was well after 1:30, and four young stomachs were churning hungrily. Molly, A.J., and Kris had each left with fifty dollars in cash, but Liam had cashed out his check, not wanting to have it inaccessible for any length of time. He suggested a trip to Gizmos, the local arcade and pizza parlor, and offered to buy lunch, for which he was lauded as the hero of the day.

The next two and a half hours were an orgy of *Asteroids*, *Joust*, *PacMan* and *Tempest*, pizza slices, soda pop and Skee-Ball. A.J. traded in his tickets on a Darth Vader Pez dispenser. Kris exchanged his for a plastic protractor and generic space alien pencil topper. Molly and Liam engaged in a battle royale for Skee-Ball supremacy, with Liam barely eking out the win. As they cashed in their tickets, Liam convinced himself she'd purposely lost the final game. Molly knew she had.

By 4 p.m., with pockets lighter in cash but bellies full of pizza and candy bars, the Calico Kids pedaled for the Wedderburn bridge and home.

It was decided en route that the group would forgo the *D&D* campaign in favor of getting some rest, and an early start Sunday morning for their follow-up investigation at Indian Bluff.

The morning swept in with a Pacific storm front that poured rain most of the day.

It was no use.

A.J. made some phone calls, watched an old monster movie with his dad, and scribbled some notes for the next *D&D* session in his room. He fell asleep early, readying himself for the final three days of school.

Track 8:
SOMEONE SOMEWHERE
(IN SUMMERTIME)
Simple Minds (1982)

Kris and A.J. passed their algebra final, Kris with a B-plus, and A.J. squeaking by with a C-minus. The last three days of eighth grade were distilled agony—one endless string of educational movies they'd already seen a hundred times, clearly programmed to keep the students quiet so the teachers could complete their final grades for the year. All A.J. and Kris could think about, as a film narrator from the early 1960s droned on about nucleotides, was getting a chance to ride out to Old Town again. It would get more difficult to be near old Calico during the summer without being discovered, as more older kids would be parking at the Bluff.

In wood shop, Liam had put the finishing touches on a one-sixteenth scale catapult. He'd initially considered a trebuchet, but the potential increase in range was overridden by the practical applications of aiming, and hitting a closer target. All three boys looked forward to trying it out in Liam's overgrown backyard against a wall of empty beer and soda cans.

Wednesday was a half-day for the eighth graders, but even then real-life obligations intruded on the plans of A.J. and the gang. There was to be a commencement at 6 p.m., celebrating their advancement to the ninth grade, and high school.

Despite being a grade behind them, Molly appeared at the graduation shindig to congratulate the boys, slipping A.J. a mix tape of New Romantic synth pop on the sly. He sneaked a look at it in the restroom. She'd named the collection *Bad Hat Harry* after a line from *Jaws*, the title artistically written and embellished with their triangular alien symbol and a multitude of stars, as ornate as an illuminated medieval manuscript. He went home and promptly put it in the cassette deck in his room, listening to it twice over before falling asleep to David Sylvian's buttery baritone on Japan's *Nightporter*.

Thursday proved to be breezy and mild. Liam began the day by phoning a coin dealer in Crescent City to see if they'd want to take the Liberty dollar off his hands. When the merchant heard the date was 1870, he offered ten thousand dollars cash, sight unseen. Liam talked him up to twenty, knowing it was worth at least fifty, and that he'd never be able to sell it for that much on his own. They settled on fifteen, and made arrangements for Liam to come down to the shop on Saturday, when A.J.'s dad or another adult could make the drive. He would actually have to bank the money this time. It was far too much cash to keep secret, and Liam didn't want his mom drinking it away. He stowed the coin away inside a "patched" section of drywall behind his bed, next to the plastic bag of weed and a ratty copy of *Penthouse* from October, 1979.

A.J., Kris, and Molly met for a lunchtime planning session at the diner before biking out to Liam's place. They took turns playing with the catapult as the day wore on, and as the sun began to set, packed up for their next excursion.

The sky was a darkening hue of orange and blood red as they crossed Perry's Bridge and headed out toward the clear cut, a strange silence connecting them like a four-way umbilical cord. Liam had left his PVC pipe behind at A.J.'s behest, despite a token protest of, "One day you'll be happy my pole is there." Molly had Bodhi's *Body Electric* mix tape in the Walkman, listening to The Vapors with the volume up.

The Bluff was empty as they approached around the curve. As the sun dipped under the tree line behind them, the four braked to a stop in the turnout, precariously near the steep hillside that separated the road from the clearcut below. The Sheriff's Department had left a few wooden sawhorse barricades with battery-powered blinkers as a warning. Teens looking for a place to make out would have to find another location for the summer.

A.J. ditched his bike on the gravel and knelt by the section of asphalt which had held the mysterious symbol only last week. The road had been gouged in a few places, but otherwise the glyph was still intact—just covered over in black spray paint.

Molly set her kickstand and approached A.J. as the other two boys looked on.

"What were they trying to do?" she asked.

A.J. shrugged, a frown taking over his expression. "Hell if I know. Maybe just cover it up until a DOT crew can come out to resurface it?"

Liam suddenly caught a fragment of sound on the evening breeze, his attention drawn back to the curve in the road. "Whoa guys, heads up."

Kris shifted on his banana seat. "Car," he added redundantly.

Liam shot him a tired glare.

They heard the distorted boom of Van Halen over woefully unqualified speakers before a pair of headlights came around the corner. A maroon Oldsmobile sedan with tan trim squealed on balding tires around the curve, fishtailing back onto the road. It roared forward and A.J.'s stomach instantly knotted into a ball as he realized who was in the car. It was much, much worse than being discovered by the sheriff.

"Damn," A.J. sighed under his breath, giving voice to what everyone was thinking.

The car belonged to Travis O'Brien's father, but Travis O'Brien's father wasn't driving it. As the massive Delta 88 screeched to a halt only scant yards from the sprayed-over symbol, the rumbling V-8 engine fell silent.

Whereas Liam was the bully of bullies at the middle school level, Travis O'Brien was a fanatic when it came to abusing underclassmen at the high school. He was a nineteen-year-old senior who had repeated his freshman year twice, which was probably where his disdain for incoming freshmen came from, as he'd had to undergo a second year of abuse of the upperclassmen in his day. O'Brien's hazings were legendary, the one saving grace being that he usually left the elementary and middle school kids alone. But

Liam, Kris, and A.J. were now officially high school freshmen, and thus viable targets.

Unable to see the car's occupants past the glare of the headlamps, A.J. hoped it was only Travis, that maybe with four-to-one odds, he wouldn't try anything. His hopes were soon dashed, as both the driver and passenger side doors clunked open, the forms of two teenage boys emerging from the haze of screaming guitars and pot smoke within, silhouetted behind the headlight beams.

"Whadda we got here, kids?" lilted a voice from the one of the silhouettes, "a camp-out?"

A.J. squinted through his glasses. That didn't sound like Travis. His stomach flipped again. That sounded like Mick Wolfsohn, O'Brien's sidekick. He knew if he made a dash for his bike to attempt a getaway, it would trigger the two older boys' prey drive, and the results would be more catastrophic than if he played it cool. But it was sure hard to play cool when there was sweat running in beads down his back.

Molly's eyes darted from A.J. to the silhouettes, which were now moving from behind the car doors, slamming them shut with a synchronized *thunk*. Kris remained on his bike, sitting on the saddle with one foot on a pedal and the other bracing against the ground like a human kickstand. Liam stood astride the

Frankenbike, gripping the handlebars through his fingerless driving gloves, casting sidelong glances over the edge of the bluff.

"I said, whadda we got here, kids?"

It was definitely Mick, providing the setup for his overlord.

"Nothing," A.J. shrugged. "Just heading back to town."

The other silhouette stepped in front of the left headlight, and they could suddenly see O'Brien's features. He was a fireplug: thick-necked and tan, with chestnut eyes that pierced the dim light, and a cruel smile displaying a comical gap in his front teeth. Dishwater blond hair was buzzed short, and his arms were the size of small tree trunks. It was no secret that O'Brien was the prize weapon on the Calico High wrestling team, which was probably why he never seemed to face any repercussions for his toxic behavior. He reeked of Acapulco Gold, Speed Stick, and privilege.

"What's the hurry, children?" O'Brien growled, thrusting his chin forward so that the ring of puka shells encircling his fleshy neck caught the orange light of sunset. His white tank top was stippled in paint and greasy fingerprints, a red flannel shirt hanging open to his well-worn Levis. "You guys just graduated junior high, didn't you? You know that means you're mine now."

"Come on, man," Liam hailed from the edge of the cliff. "Leave 'em alone."

O'Brien shifted his focus from A.J. to Liam, who was as tall as he was, if not as packed with solid muscle. "Leave *them* alone?" he shot back. "*Them*? Who says you're not *them*?"

A.J. nervously shifted his weight back and forth. He could now see Mick, O'Brien's slightly smaller, darker-complected doppelganger. The seventeen-year-old was clad in a KISS concert tee and camo Army jacket, black work boots untied. His coal-black hair was feathered, and he'd been smoking so much weed that he literally smelled like a skunk had sprayed him.

"We just wanna get back to town," A.J. quietly protested.

O'Brien's brow furrowed as if puzzling a brain-busting math problem. "But...why?" he asked. "What's the hurry?"

A.J. glanced down, noticing for the first time that he was standing dead center in the sprayed-over glyph. His face was clammy, and the color had drained from his cheeks. He wished he could be somewhere else—*anywhere* else but right there.

"Yeah," Mick repeated. "What's the hurry?"

As he spoke, Liam flung the Frankenbike directly at O'Brien, dashing across the front of the Olds to land a powerful right cross on Mick's jaw. Mick reeled but returned to stance, throwing Liam aside by his jacket front so that the younger boy sprawled into the street. O'Brien grabbed the bike frame as it came toward him, dropping it to follow Liam's trajectory as Mick cocked an arm back to strike at A.J. Out of instinct, A.J. dropped to the ground, his bare palms contacting the sprayed-over sigil.

A powerful strobe of light erupted from seemingly everywhere at once, a flash that threatened to blind everyone in the vicinity. Hands flew to faces to block the assault as a gust of wind rushed into the turnout. All eyes squinted to readjust, glancing from person to person, and ultimately down to the asphalt.

A.J. was gone.

Track 9:
WAIT FOR THE BLACKOUT
The Damned (1979)

"——the hell?"

Mick's eyes darted like guppies in a pet shop plastic bag. His target had completely vanished in front of him. Pivoting almost like a basketball player, he glanced at Molly, then Kris. "What is this?"

His question was met by a chorus of silent shrugs. Kris and Molly couldn't even believe their own eyes, much less educate the older boys on what had happened.

O'Brien approached the sprayed-over glyph and gave Mick a casual shove. "What the shit, man?"

A cloud began to spread across Mick's face. He considered the possibility that the last blunt he and O'Brien shared could have been laced with something. "I dunno, man! He just disappeared!"

"Bullshit, dude. Nobody just *disappears*!" O'Brien punctuated the point by slugging his buddy in the shoulder.

Kris felt the gears in his head turning. Eric and Jeannie had disappeared from Indian Bluff, and both had turned up in different places in Old Town. His heart climbed into his throat, causing him to swallow hard in the sudden realization. Molly found his gaze, and her eyes widened with his in unison.

The glyph was a teleportation device.

Mick winced and continued to look around the area for any clue as to A.J.'s whereabouts.

Molly looked back at the two older teens, eyebrow raised, as O'Brien turned his attention toward Liam, who was just staggering to his feet.

"Where'd your friend go, loser?"

Though flustered, Liam was used to bigger, older aggressors, and from his experience with his mom's endless queue of boyfriends, he knew how to take a beating. He also could give as good as he got. O'Brien outweighed him by fifty pounds, but they were just about equal in height. It was worth a shot, if only to try out the moves he'd gleaned from all those Bruce Lee films he watched late at night in his bedroom.

He feinted a right cross at O'Brien's head, and the older boy's hands flew up unconsciously to protect his face. Bringing a booted foot up into O'Brien's groin, he waited for the requisite whimper and collapse, which never came.

Liam glanced down and he saw that O'Brien had caught his foot in a block between two hands. The older boy turned, taking Liam's foot with him. There was a grotesque pop, then Liam was flung to the ground where A.J. had disappeared.

Another blinding blast of white light erupted from everywhere at once.

CR

A.J. opened his eyes in almost complete darkness, head swimming, wrist throbbing from where he'd landed on the ground.

He felt himself try to stand. A distant gray light rushed past his field of vision, and he doubled over, trying desperately not to vomit. Hunched forward with hands on his knees, the boy breathed deeply, intentionally—in through the nose, out through the mouth—until at last he felt stable.

He realized the dim light was actually above him, and wasn't actually moving at all.

The motion had been his own head reeling. Slowly turning in a full circle, he found he was squatting on some sort of raised metal plate or dais, the familiar alien glyph illuminated within. It was a large enough radius to stand in, glowing a soft white-blue in the otherwise dark environment.

Aside from the illumination above and below, there was no other light. No wind, not so much as a slight breeze. The air was completely still, which consequently made it stuffy as hell. He stood from his front crouch and gathered his bearings.

He stood in a column of soft light, surrounded by darkness, in what he assumed was a room of some kind. Managing a tentative, "H-hello?" A.J. waited for a reply, but none came.

C33

Liam rolled to a sitting position and opened his eyes. Wherever he was, it was pitch black. The occasional *plink* of a falling water droplet echoed through what was clearly some sort of large, cavernous environment. His stomach heaved and forced him to take a moment. The pain in his right ankle was agony, and he winced as he fished the disposable Bic lighter from one of the myriad array of pants pockets.

The mechanism was tight and took several tries before a tiny flame extended from the top.

Liam squinted, scanning the interior of what appeared to be a cave of some kind. But as his eyes adjusted to the tiny amount of illumination, he began to discern some detail. It wasn't merely a natural hollow. The walls of the cavern didn't appear to be of a tectonic origin. Relatively symmetric gouges and grooves hinted at man-made beginnings. The century-old timbers spanning the ceiling and running across upright beams into the dark corridor were another giveaway.

Liam swallowed stale air and blinked in disbelief.

He was in the Old Town silver mine.

"Well," he muttered to himself, "this is... something."

☙

Mick and O'Brien stood gobsmacked in the turnout, the Oldsmobile's headlamps illuminating a concerning state of affairs. They were now two teens fewer than mere moments ago.

Molly had backed toward her bike, and was already thinking about the best approach into Old Town. With the car blocking the road, there was really only one path before them…or rather behind them. She and Kris gave each other a silent nod.

"What the goddamn…?" O'Brien stalked the turnout, rage starting to possess his entire demeanor. Boots scuffed back and forth across the asphalt.

Mick merely turned in place, trying to spy where the other boys had perhaps hidden. His vision snapped from place to place, doing its best to register a modicum of reality.

O'Brien in the road.

Car headlights.

That other boy and girl.

O'Brien in the road.

Car headlights.

Empty bluff.

Mick caught himself in a double-take, re-scanning the edge of the turnout. "Hey!"

O'Brien jogged to get a vantage over the cliff, letting loose an expletive-laden broadside at his rapidly-vanishing quarry.

Molly and Kris careened down the hillside, faster than either had ever gone before, trailing a thin cloud of dust from each rear tire. The sun had fully set, a waning crescent moon starting to peek over the dilapidated ruins of old Calico. The two high school bullies wouldn't be able to follow them down the hillside in the Olds without seriously risking damage to the front end and possibly the engine as well. A distant squeal of tires told them that the older boys were either hightailing it back home, or continuing on the North Bank frontage road to the entrance of Old Town, perhaps in an effort to cut them off. Regardless, Kris and Molly were almost guaranteed to reach the mid-point of the old Main Street before O'Brien could get there.

"Where are we going?" Kris huffed, the rumbling of the uneven ground vibrating up through his ribcage.

Molly stood on her pedals, pumping them with all her might. "Old Town. The livery stable, where we found Eric."

CR

A.J. reappeared within the glyph at Indian Bluff just as O'Brien's car fishtailed down the road toward Old Town. If there'd been a flash, the bullies had made no indication of having seen it.

He felt queasy again, his insides doing cartwheels as he tried to get his bearings.

The road was dark. Liam's bike was on its side against one of the blinking hazard signs.

A.J.'s was where he'd left it. And everyone was gone.

Wait a minute. How had he teleported back here?

He wracked his brain, trying to recall the series of events: He'd thought about stepping off the raised platform, considered stepping out of the column of light. But then he'd remembered a last-minute hesitation, and thought he would much rather be back with his friends. Then he'd reached down and touched the glyph with his left hand.

Back with his friends! At the Bluff!

"Aha!" A.J. smiled to himself, thinking he was finally in mental possession of the key.

Closing his eyes, he pictured all three of his friends' faces, crouched inside the painted-over glyph, and touched the asphalt. He didn't register the strobe effect of the teleportation, but he noticed an immediate shift in air pressure and ambient temperature. A small, flickering light was visible to his left, and he recognized the young man holding it.

"Liam!" he gasped, crouching over again as another wave of nausea hit.

Liam jumped and turned to face him. "Holy shit, A.J.!"

Molly and Kris skidded to a halt beside the livery, ditching their bikes in the shadow of the rickety building. They moved in silent unison to the rear corner, peeking around to look both ways up and down Main Street.

Perhaps a hundred yards distant, they could see the play of headlights across the line of barricades.

"We can't let them find us," Molly said, and no sooner had the words left her mouth than the quick growl of a police siren blared from behind the Olds. A second set of headlights appeared, along with a blinking blue and red light bar atop the Sheriff's Department Bronco.

The bullies were thwarted. If it was Sheriff Chavez in the truck, she might catch a whiff of them and escort them to Gold Beach for a night in jail. If it was Halverson, they'd be pointed back home to town with a warning. In either case, they wouldn't be a further impediment tonight. They watched the Oldsmobile headlights back away and turn toward the road, followed by the flashing red and blue. They froze in tableau for a solid couple of minutes before finding the will to move.

"Should we check inside?" Kris asked, more in an attempt to psych himself up to do it, rather than an actual inquiry.

"Duh," Molly replied, already heading toward the wrecked door they'd helped Eric Somerville through less than a week previous. She shrugged an arm out of the backpack she carried, unzipping the main partition to produce a plastic household flashlight. Flicking it on, she aimed the beam through the splintered boards and antique iron work, roaming it over the floor where their alien symbol was still visible. "Shape's still there," Molly announced quietly, "but nobody's home."

Kris exhaled, visibly relieved. He glanced up Main Street to the north and his breath caught again. He reached out, tugging at Molly's sweatshirt. "Hey," he whispered, little more than a hiss. "Hey. Molly."

"What?" Molly turned, switching off the flashlight so as not to be seen.

Kris gestured at a bobbing point of light at the mouth of the mine entrance. Shadows played across the interior walls, telling them someone was up there.

"Whoa," Molly uttered to herself. Before Kris could gather another thought, she'd put her arm through the strap of the backpack, and was off toward the mine.

"Hey," he wheezed, at too low a volume to be heard. He swallowed a dry gulp of dusty air, glancing to the south, then behind across the clearcut to Indian Bluff. Faced with the choice to remain with the bikes in the middle of a spooky ghost town with little to no moon-light, or follow Molly, Kris gathered his courage and headed off after her.

Track 10:
TWIST & CRAWL
The English Beat (1980)

"So that's where you went!" Molly exclaimed, more excited than she let on.

Liam and A.J. paused on the bent cart rails. There was the scratch of a lighter igniting, and Liam raised the flame to illuminate Molly at the top of the incline at the mine entrance. Kris pulled to a stop behind her, breathing hard.

A.J. sighed in relief. "Dude. You have no idea..."

"What did you find?" Molly flicked on the flashlight and pushed past the boys, ambling into the timber-lined corridor.

"We um..." A.J. stammered, following her into the mine. "Wait!"

It was Liam's turn to roll his eyes. He hobbled after A.J., and was surprised when Kris ducked under his arm and grabbed him around the waist to help.

It was only a short trek to the antechamber where Liam and A.J. had teleported, Molly's light showing off a great slab of flat granite, the strange geometric symbol still seared into it. It looked to be about the same radius as the shape in the livery stable, as well as the one at the bluff.

"What do we do?" Molly asked.

A.J. stood, hands on hips, his brain still swimming from the events of the past ten minutes. "Huh?"

Molly threw him a patronizing look. "How do you work it? You and Liam friggin' disappeared. And obviously it popped you out here."

"It popped me out here," Liam interjected, limping into the side room with an arm across Kris' shoulder. "But A.J. went somewhere else first."

Molly was instantly intrigued. "Somewhere else?"

A.J. nodded. "Yeah."

"Where?"

"I'm not sure. It was dark, and um...a column of light...and I didn't want to step outside."

Molly tilted the flashlight under A.J.'s chin and locked eyes with him. "How do you make it work?"

"I...I'm pretty sure you have to be thinking of a place, and then you touch the symbol with your bare skin, and it takes you to the symbol closest to where you wanted to go."

A grin crept across Molly's face, and her eyes lit up almost maniacally. "Let's try it together!"

"What?" Kris gasped, almost dropping Liam.

A.J. held up a hand. "Wait, we don't even know if it works like that."

Molly grabbed his hand, pulling him onto the glyph on the stone slab. This was happening, and it was happening right now. A.J. made a show of hesitancy, but in truth, he was just as anxious to try it again.

The air was damp and tinged with the smell of mossy earth. They stood together inside the shape, senses elevated, adrenaline surging. She faced him, finding his gaze, holding his left hand firmly in her right. "Think of the mystery place," she said softly. "The column of light."

A.J. nodded. "Got it."

Still clutching his hand tightly, Molly guided them both to a crouch, their gaze never breaking.

A.J. extended his right hand, index finger brushing the granite.

Kris and Liam clamped their eyes shut reflexively as the flash exploded across every surface of the chamber. This time Liam noticed a slight whoosh of air filling a vacuum, and the tiniest smell of ozone.

"I guess we wait?" Kris asked.

Liam sighed, ankle still throbbing. "Yep."

The room was completely dark as A.J. had described, save for the gray light above, and the illumination from the symbol below.

Molly gradually raised her head and saw A.J.'s brown eyes staring back at her. She wasn't sure if the queasy feeling in her stomach was nausea, adolescent proximity to a boy, or raw excitement about the mystery unfolding in front of them.

A.J. turned his head, leaning over and heaving over the edge of the platform.

Molly sighed. It was apparently just nausea.

She started to stand, but her sense of balance was off, and she stumbled. A.J. caught her on his way up.

"Easy there," he huffed. "It's a bit disorienting at first."

Molly chuckled. "At first? You're the one tossing cookies."

"Yeah, well this is my third time in about ten minutes, so..."

"Okay, hotshot," Molly retorted, aiming her flashlight around the dark space outside the glyph platform.

It seemed to be a circular room, maybe twenty feet across, with a concrete floor and acoustic panels lining the walls. In the middle of the panels stood a heavy office door. The space was otherwise unfurnished and unoccupied.

Molly was already off the platform and halfway to the door. "Come on!"

A.J. winced. Were they really going to go exploring a completely unknown environment, with half their group back in Old Town, who knows how far away?

Yes. Yes they were.

Molly leaned an ear against the door and listened for a few moments as A.J. caught up with her. "Sounds clear," she said.

As she cracked the door open to peek outside, A.J. noticed for the first time how close he was standing. Molly noticed too.

"Your breath smells like puke," she muttered. "Take a piece of gum—small pocket of the backpack."

Refocusing on the pack, A.J. unzipped the rearmost chamber, fishing out a small brick of watermelon Bubble Yum. He pinched the block-shaped piece from within, zipped the backpack, and shoved the pink gum into his mouth.

Artificial watermelon was somewhat better than the taste of vomit.

Molly slinked out the door, pulling A.J. with her before he had time to protest. They found themselves in a bland, nondescript office hallway, a room full of vacant cubicles to the right, another hall to the left, terminating at an identical door. A low bank of metal file cabinets lined the wall across from the cube farm. Fluorescent ceiling light fixtures remained dark. The entire place was empty and silent, save for the quiet rustling of A.J. and Molly and their backpacks.

"What the hell is this place?" Molly asked.

A.J. glanced back at the door to the room they'd teleported into. A plaque placed in the center, at adult eye level, was printed with a stylized illustration of a black bird of prey, head to the side, wings outstretched, talons extended. It struck A.J. as both tribal in nature and "official" or "governmental". As he cataloged the information, he realized Molly had let go his hand and was already heading toward the opposite door. "Molly!" he hissed. "Wait up!"

As they tiptoed to a stop at the far end of the corridor, A.J. noticed an identical plaque on the door. "Black eagle," he whispered.

Molly frowned. "What?"

"The picture. It's a black eagle."

"What does it mean?"

"I don't know," A.J. shrugged, glancing down at the door handle and realizing there was no expanded security. No card-reader, no keypad, just a lever handle. He tested it, pushing down the handle and gingerly leaning the door open.

Both A.J. and Molly had seen their share of science fiction movies in their young years, and the room they stepped into was straight out of one of them. It was a giant technical bay, easily sixty feet across, with computer terminal workstations and refrigerator-sized mainframe computers lining the outer walls. A metal access door thirty feet wide sat closed at the far end. In the center of the bay stood some kind of vehicle that A.J. felt could only be described as a spaceship.

It was circular, with a bay of windows along one side, and what looked like entry doors on either side and at the rear, opposite the forward view ports. Painted in various pale gray tones with red highlights, it seemed constructed of molded plastic as opposed to metal. The warning decals and hazard stripes likewise gave it a quite terrestrial feel—not alien at all.

"Holy shit," A.J. gawped. Every fiber of his being was on alert, his brain locked in a loop: *We shouldn't be here. We shouldn't be here.*

Molly shined her light across the side of the craft, illuminating exquisite construction and design. "What is it, you think?"

"I dunno, man. I don't even know where we are. This could be a government black ops site, some kind of UFO research facility..."

A.J. realized her question had been largely rhetorical when he heard the roll of a file cabinet being opened, and glanced over his shoulder to see Molly in the hallway, pawing through various folders within.

"Molly, what are you—? Hey, don't get into that stuff..."

"Look at this," Molly said, seemingly unsurprised at her discoveries. "Eric Somerville. And here's a file on Jeannie Wells." She pulled the folders from their hangers within, rifling through the contents. "Huh. There's barely anything on them—just vitals, personal data and a mugshot. Nothing about what they were doing with them here."

Here, A.J. repeated in his mind. *We shouldn't be here.*

"Molly, put those back!" he hissed in a loud whisper, to no avail. "We're gonna get caught!"

As if on cue, a distant knock erupted from deep within the complex, and dim red lights flicked on. They could hear the low rumble of large diesel engines outside the place.

"Uh oh," Molly frowned. "Daddy's home." Quickly shoving the folders back into the file cabinet, she flicked off her flashlight and turned toward the sound of the vehicles outside.

This time it was A.J.'s turn to grab Molly's hand, leading the charge from the vehicle hangar and back down the corridor.

The sound of heavy corrugated steel doors rolling up reverberated through the halls. Whoever owned this place had indeed returned, in force. Neither A.J. nor Molly wanted to stick around to find out who it was.

They slipped back into the teleportation room and rushed to the dais, stepping into the column of light. A.J. still clutched Molly's hand.

"Think of the mine," he instructed.

"You think of the mine," she scolded. "I'm just along for the ride."

Kneeling into a crouch, A.J. closed his eyes and imagined Kris and Liam waiting for them in the cave. Then he touched his hand to the symbol beneath them.

Track 11:
DO THE DARK

Blondie (1980)

Another blinding strobe of light, a subtle pop of air readjusting to the local ambient pressure, and A.J. and Molly appeared on the granite.

"Holy shit," Kris exclaimed, blinking in disbelief. So far, he'd watched three of his friends disappear—one of them twice! Two had vanished mere minutes ago and reappeared just now, and Kris was finding that it never got old.

A.J. staggered upright as Molly expelled the contents of her stomach in the corner of the cave. "You guys," he huffed.

"What happened?" Liam demanded.

"Let's get back, and I'll tell you."

When Molly had recovered from the nausea, a fresh cube of Bubble Yum between her teeth, the four friends made their way down the blasted tunnel to the mine entrance. Kris and A.J. acted as human crutches for Liam, who hadn't yet been curious enough to remove his boot and check the damage to his ankle. It didn't feel broken, but there was definitely at least a sprain.

As they worked their way slowly down the long grade to Old Town, Liam's leg became fatigued to the point of anger. By the time they reached the teetering old livery stable, where Kris and Molly's bikes were stashed, he was grimacing in agony.

"Guys, stop," he winced. "I can't."

"We still have to get up to the bluff to the other bikes," Kris complained.

Molly jutted out a slender hip. "Or do we?" she pondered.

A.J. stared blankly at her. "Really?"

"What."

"You just puked in the mines."

"So?"

"You like this way too much."

Molly stood in front of the boys like a schoolteacher, hands on hips. "Look. We've all been to the bluff. We know what it looks like. We know it'll teleport our clothes and stuff." She waved the plastic flashlight in demonstration. "I'll even go first."

As the three boys watched with mouths like goldfish, Molly packed away the flashlight and walked her bike over the perimeter of old timbers outside the livery, treading delicately on the dirt floor as she disappeared inside. When she was completely within the boundaries of the shape on the floor, bike and all, she thought of the view from Indian Bluff, and knelt down to touch the ground.

The flash was visible from outside the stables.

Glancing to the southwest and what seemed to be a lightning strike at the bluff, the boys watched as a small flashlight beam flicked on and waved to them in the distance.

A.J. sighed, nodding. This was clearly the easiest way to get Liam back to his bike. "Okay, Kris," he said, gesturing at the crumbled stable door. "You're next."

Kris gave him a look of abject terror, and A.J. realized he was the only remaining member of this little gang who hadn't actually teleported yet.

"Here," A.J. amended. "Maybe we can all fit inside the glyph."

The boys padded carefully into the stable, Liam hobbling between them. As A.J. had posited, the limits of the shape were large enough to contain the three of them and the Kricycle.

"Hold onto me," A.J. instructed. "Think of the bluff. Think of Molly."

They knelt in unison, each with a hand on A.J., Kris gripping his bike's handlebars as well.

Molly clamped her eyes shut as the silent lightning flashed before her. All three boys knelt in the turnout. Kris wobbled a bit, then tripped over his bike as he retched onto the asphalt.

Molly had already retrieved Liam's Frankenbike, offering the handlebars as A.J. helped him toward it. She noticed Kris wiping his mouth on his sweatshirt sleeve and giggled.

"Pretty cool, huh?" she winked, tossing him a piece of watermelon Bubble Yum.

Liam allowed the distraction to obscure the pain in his ankle. "Oh dude, lemme have some."

Molly grinned, prying the last piece from the glossy foil wrapper and holding it out like a golden relic. "Who's rad?"

Liam chuckled. "You are."

"Say it."

"You're rad."

He started to grab it, but Molly pulled it away.

"Who's the *Asteroids* master?"

"You're the *Asteroids* master."

Smiling sweetly, Molly opened her hand, allowing Liam to take the gum. "Who's your buddy?"

Liam unwrapped the pink cube from the paper and shoved it in his mouth. "*Mowwyf mah bubby.*"

"Damn straight."

It took Kris a minute to regain his footing, swaying and wobbling as if standing in a row-boat.

The four friends pedaled back to town in complete silence, hyper-aware of any sign of headlights that might indicate the presence of high school bullies, local police, or mysterious black government vehicles.

They arrived at Liam's house first, helping him get settled with a bag of frozen corn on his ankle. His mom was out, apparently with a new boyfriend, Paul. The note on the fridge said they'd be in Crescent City overnight, and she'd be back in time for her shift at the bar on Friday.

Fortunately she'd stocked the fridge with cokes and frozen pizzas.

As the kitchen expert, Kris threw a couple pizzas in the pastel yellow oven and tossed cans of soda to everyone as they settled in the main living area. Molly sat on the brick fire-place hearth, and A.J. took up a spot on a floral print sofa from the late 1960s.

A.J. and Molly told the group about the industrial office complex they'd explored a mere fraction of, including the black eagle placards and what appeared to be a government-built UFO. She described the files on Jeannie and Eric, complete with mugshots that revealed a state of catatonia. There was precious little information in the files otherwise—just basic physical statistics, addresses, and telephone numbers.

A.J. thanked Molly for returning the folders and their contents to the file cabinet. They did not want to be caught with classified government files from a secret installation.

Liam asked more about the ship. Kris posited that there could be a connection between the UFO and the black car which had tried to run them down last week. A chorus of blank stares was the response.

A.J. blinked at him. "Really? You think?"

"Well," Kris protested, "what are we gonna do?"

Liam shifted uncomfortably in the wicker papasan chair, his swollen foot propped on a milk crate, frozen corn draped across the ankle. "Dude, what you guys found is a friggin' black ops site."

"That's what I mean," Kris insisted. "What are we gonna do about it?"

"What do you mean, *What are we gonna do about it?*' It's a black ops site. We're a group of teenagers from the sticks. If they wanted to, they could make us disappear."

A.J. cast his eyes down at the brown shag carpet and sighed. "You're right. He's right, guys."

Molly took a swig of cola from the red can and looked from face to face. Kris stood with his butt leaning against the Formica bar counter outside the kitchen, holding his soda can at belly height. He was silent.

A.J. bobbed his head back and forth like a chicken, something he did automatically when convincing himself of a course of action. "We pushed our luck today. We push it any more, and we could get in a lot of trouble. And not the regular kind of trouble. We need to play it cool, keep our heads down, stay on the west side of the clearcut. No more trips out to Old Town." He took a gulp from his own can and thought for a moment. "And that's okay. We found Jeannie and Eric, and we know how they disappeared..."

Kris interrupted, pointing at the inside of his wrist. "But they had those brands—"

"I'm sure it had something to do with the complex we found," A.J. retorted. "Maybe they were experimented on, who knows?"

Molly shrugged. "The files didn't say."

"We should talk to them," Kris suggested.

"We did," Liam shot back. "They didn't remember anything."

A.J. set his soda can on a wood laminate side table. "There's nothing we can do," he said with finality. "I know, it's hard to believe that came out of my mouth. But if we value our lives, we need to keep quiet about this. At least for a while."

A silent minute passed among the four friends, everyone lost in their own thoughts. Finally A.J. picked up his can. "We've got a whole summer to hang out," he said, taking a swallow. "We've got reward money to spend."

Liam raised his can in a mock toast. "Yeah buddy." Then his eyes went wide as multiple realizations hit his brain in a cascade of excitement. "Hey, I need a ride into Crescent City to sell my Liberty dollar, and there's that new Spielberg flick that opens tomorrow, and we should go. We should all go. Who wants to go?"

The brain dump was a lot, but everyone parsed it at their own pace.

"*E.T.*?" Molly perked up, a smile finding her face again after all the doom and gloom. "Totally. I'm in."

A.J. noted the bag of frozen corn on Liam's foot. "You gonna be mobile?"

Liam's smile persisted. "No, genius. Also, *Crescent City*. Thus, a ride being necessary."

"I'll talk to Bodhi," Molly suggested. "He can probably drive us."

A.J. repeated the chicken motion with his head. "Cool. Cool."

"To the uncanny Calico commandos," Liam proposed, raising the Coke can a second time and speaking in an archaic movie villain tone. "Let us never speak of Project Black Eagle in public."

Although only Kris had ever actually been a Cub Scout, they all held up the two-finger salute, and repeated, "Never."

Molly giggled, gently turning the soda can around in her hand. "Like you even know what 'uncanny' means..."

Track 12:
DAYLIGHT TITANS

The Vapors (1980)

Liam's ankle healed within a week, and then summer passed like a fast-cut montage in a Sam Raimi film. Although the group stuck close to town for the rest of June, they began to range farther afield during July and August. Breakfast at the diner, planning out the checklist for the day, helping Kris clean up after his shift so he could join them sooner. They biked into Gold Beach several times a week, blowing their reward money at Gizmo's arcade, and catching every new genre movie that came through the Redwood Theater in nearby Brookings, although sometimes they'd have to drive to Medford or Grant's Pass to catch the less mainstream stuff.

They quietly wept when E.T. died, cheered in their seats when he came back to life, and threw each other knowing looks when the kids outran the feds on their bikes. They rooted for

Admiral Kirk to outwit the superior intellect of Khan and his wrath. They dug their fingers into their legs through most of *Poltergeist* and *The Thing*, and had their minds blown by *Blade Runner* and *Tron* and *The Wall*.

Ordinarily, Molly wouldn't have been able to get into an R-rated movie like *Blade Runner*, but Liam's mom had a strong guilt complex and didn't have a problem with purchasing the tickets at the box office and leaving the kids at the theater to enjoy themselves. A.J. and Kris had used that very method to join Liam at showings of *Conan the Barbarian* and *The Road Warrior* back in May.

And if Ms. Scott wasn't available, Molly's brother Bodhi could usually be convinced with a free movie ticket. He was seventeen, tall and attractive, and had procured a fake ID in Eugene just before the end of the previous school year. Not once did movie theater personnel ever question his presence among a group of thirteen- and fourteen-year-olds at an R-rated film.

Weekdays were split among matinees, arcade time and relaxing on the river. Nights were for indoctrinating Molly into the wonders of *Dungeons & Dragons*. Although hesitant to fully commit at first, she eventually took to it like a duck to water, and by the end of summer had even dungeon-mastered her first campaign. A.J. welcomed the opportunity to play a character, rather than running the game all the time. The group even stepped outside their fantasy milieu to dip their collective toe in an espionage roleplaying game called *Top Secret*, which everyone seemed to enjoy except A.J., who felt it was just too real.

Molly continued their musical education through the mix tapes in Bodhi's collection, or cassettes she received in the mail from old friends in L.A. The Clash's *Combat Rock* was among them, an album Liam instantly fell in love with, borrowed, and never returned. He made up for it with dubbed copies of Van Halen's *Diver Down* and Iron Maiden's *The Number of the Beast*.

The four were as good as their word. No one ventured out to Indian Bluff or Old Town for the rest of the summer. An occasional sighting of Sheriff Chavez or Deputy Halverson in Gold Beach was the extent of their interaction with local law enforcement. They mostly stayed off the streets at night, content to trade off sleeping over at each other's houses.

Molly was the lone exception, subject to old-fashioned notions of propriety on her parents' part. Although her original arrival in the group had upset the apple cart with a dangerous injection of estrogen in the teenage boys' club, their friendship had matured into a full and casual acceptance.

She had truly become "one of the guys".

Occasionally, Bodhi and his fifteen-year-old girlfriend Chlöe would hang out with the gang, which made A.J. and Kris feel especially mature and important.

It certainly helped that Molly's parents owned the nicest house in Calico—a large Craftsman home that in times past might have been called a mansion, and had spent some time as a boarding house and B&B before the Reynolds family had purchased it, moving their real estate business up from southern California. The entire daylight basement had been converted to a "rumpus room", a recreation area paneled in tongue-and-groove cedar, with a full-size pool table and beanbag sitting area which featured a color television and Atari game console.

Many summer nights were spent in the Reynolds family rec room, and the boys were even allowed to stay over because Molly had her own bedroom and there was parental, or older brother, supervision.

They'd gotten lucky during June and July in regard to Travis O'Brien and Mick Wulf-sohn. Travis apparently had gotten a job in the cannery, and Mick was sweeping floors at the pulp mill. The time Mick and Travis were out cruising was usually when the four friends were inside, slaying imaginary trolls and dragons. But as August closed out and everyone prepared for the new school year, a looming dread descended over the four friends, or at least the three boys entering high school. The trolls and dragons would no longer be imaginary, which A.J. learned on day one, when Mick caught him in the men's restroom and shoved his head in a toilet.

Bodhi went to bat for A.J. and the other boys as often as he could, but as a senior who had to navigate his own high school career, including football stardom, dating, and college prep, he simply couldn't be everywhere at once. Fortunately, Bodhi's influence seemed to be enough to get the two bullies to de-escalate somewhat, at least for most of September.

As autumn settled into the Rogue River Valley, life found a new rhythm. Calico High's football team beat Eagle Point in the homecoming game, and the overall sentiment among the Lumberjacks student body was an optimistic one.

Then October arrived, and with it came the ghosts.

It was the habit of Grandmother Korolewski to bake seasonal cookies, her specialty during the fall being pumpkin. Kris was used to the tradition, and even if blindfolded and kept in a windowless room, could tell the time of year by sampling one of *Babciu*'s cookies. On Saturday the 23rd, after a slow afternoon at the diner, Kris prepared to join the *D&D* game at Molly's, stopping in the kitchen to grab a warm pumpkin cookie from the stack and kiss his grandmother goodbye.

He found the old woman rolling out what appeared to be her fifth or perhaps sixth batch of dough on the counter. She watched him take the cookie and nodded.

"Things different this autumn," she said cryptically.

"How do you mean, *Babciu*?" Kris grabbed a few extras for the group, going to a drawer and slipping them into a zip-lock bag.

"The lines of the river," she answered, casting her gaze upward with her single white eye. "Energy is different."

Kris could usually chalk up his grandmother's fortune cookie wisdom to the trauma of being a Holocaust survivor, but this time her demeanor was far more serious. It gave him pause, and he joined her across the island, a quizzical expression as he chewed. "Different how?"

"Awakened," she warned. "Spirits walk."

Kris swallowed his bite. "Hold up. 'Spirits walk'? What spirits?"

She eyed her grandson as he took another bite of cookie, pointing at the side of her head to illustrate. "You will see."

Kris was starting to feel nervous, but tried to shake it off.

"You know how to repel spirits, yes?"

The boy shook his head.

"Like in the Old Country. I show you later."

Her smile was somewhat creepy and full of questionable dentistry, but it was earnest. "You go play with your friends now," she instructed, waving him toward the back door. "Go. Have fun."

Slowly, Kris readjusted his brain to mundane function and pushed open the door, and Grandma suddenly pointed a bony, withered finger at him.

"But beware the spirits!"

He jumped, turning back to see his ancient grandmother, white-haired and wrinkled, with her strange eye and bad teeth, pointing an accusatory talon at him.

"I will, *Babciu*," he assured.

"Okay then," she said, returning immediately to rolling out her cookie dough, as if nothing about the past five minutes had been even remotely strange.

Kris turned away and exited the diner, going to where his bike was chained to a carport column. He tossed the plastic bag of treats in the front milk crate basket and undid the combination lock by rote. Throwing his leg over the frame to sit on the saddle, Kris shoved a second cookie into his mouth, pushed off from the carport slab and angled his bike up Durham Street. Evening traffic was light, with only a few cars and almost no people out and about.

He saw the first ghost in the middle of the street at the intersection of Durham and Third.

The apparition took the form of a Tututni brave, clad in deerskin and holding a war club at his side. It seemed to hover about six inches above the ground, feet and legs indistinct below the knees, where it became a shimmering, semi-transparent image, almost a silent movie projected on a glass window.

Kris skidded to a halt, pulling the uneaten portion of cookie from his mouth to inspect it. It tasted no different from any other fall batch of his grandmother's pumpkin cookies. He was certain she hadn't laced them with hallucinogens. She wasn't the type. At least he *thought* she wasn't the type. But now that he was watching a dead Tututni warrior glide down the middle of the street at sunset, he wasn't entirely sure.

The brave made no apparent notice of Kris as he walked the bike forward from the saddle, skirting well around the spirit. He kept a wary eye on the ghostly form as he crept forward, putting ever more distance between them.

Then he turned his head to face forward, let out a small shriek, and the last bit of cookie dropped from his mouth to the gutter.

He was surrounded by phantoms.

Track 13:
THE DAMNED DON'T CRY
Visage (1982)

"**Y**ou saw a *what?*" A.J. demanded, as Molly and Liam crowded in from the left and right.

Kris swallowed without a drop of saliva to coat his throat, making a sickly, sticky noise. "G...ghost. I think."

"You mean like the ones we saw at Old Town back in June?" Molly's eyes were wide, and the smile on her face told Kris she was far more into this than he was.

Despite the warm and familiar surroundings of Molly's basement rec room, Kris didn't feel particularly warm or familiar.

"Um...I...I think so?"

"What did it look like?" Liam asked, punctuated by a voluminous belch caused by the root beer he'd been nursing the past half hour. The burp sounded like a Mack truck grinding a gear, and drew everyone's attention, which pleased Liam immensely. He feigned ignorance with a shrug and an innocent, "What?," but his dark eyes were smiling under the mirrored aviator glasses he wore inside to hide the evidence of having found his mom's pot stash that morning.

Kris wasn't sure how to describe what he'd seen in any kind of rational way, so he defaulted to how a five-year-old child would tell a parent about a dream.

"It looked like an Indian...like the ones you see pictures of in the visitor's center at the state park...and I could tell he had blood running down the side of his head, but he didn't look solid, like see-through, y'know? And his legs didn't go all the way down...at least I couldn't see them...they just kind of disappeared. He had a war club, and he looked like an old black-and-white photo. And when I looked forward again, there was a ton of 'em. Indians, pioneers, lumberjacks, miners..." Kris took a deep breath and swallowed. "And kids."

A.J. had experienced too much weirdness in his own life to dismiss his friend's experience outright, but he needed more detail. This was a full-blown supernatural event in a public place. Someone else had to have seen it. "Was anyone else in the area?" he asked.

Kris shook his head. "Nah. Just a couple cars that were already turning onto Third." He shivered, hugging his shoulders tightly. "And besides," he added, "I think you have to eat the cookie to see them."

The other three kids exchanged a look that was somewhere between surprise at hearing that combination of words and complete bewilderment at the lack of context.

"Hold up," Liam said, his interest suddenly more than casual amusement. "You got some *special* cookies? You dog!"

"It's not like that," Kris protested. "*Babciu* makes these pumpkin cookies every year. It's like a recipe from the Old Country with a New World flavor—it's like her tribute to America or something. But I've been eating them all my life, and they've never done this before." He met the gaze of each of his friends in turn, locking eyes so they'd know he was dead serious—except for Liam, who still hid behind the aviators. But Kris could at least see his own expression in the mirrored lenses, and was satisfied he looked grave enough. "She's been really weird this fall," he revealed quietly. "Going on about planets aligning and energies manifesting."

"You mean beyond what the government has going on out at Old Town?" A.J. prompted-ed.

Liam wasn't having that. "Dude, that wasn't *just* the government. That shape is from an alien alphabet—we saw it in the books. And what does it have to do with the spirits we saw out there, and Kris saw tonight? This shit is bigger than the government."

"You think the government is conjuring ghosts out in an abandoned mine?" Molly retreated to the wet bar in the corner and drew a Pepsi from the mini-fridge beneath the counter. "What for?"

"Not just in the mines," Kris reminded them. "Midtown Calico, sunset."

Molly nodded, acknowledging the point, but reiterated: "What for?"

Liam slammed the last swallow from the root beer can and crumpled it for effect. "I'm just saying it's bigger than any secret government agency. If anything, their experiments with teleportation might have caused some kind of tear in the space-time continuum."

A.J. waved a hand dismissively. "Man, you've been waiting for an excuse to say 'space-time continuum' since they took *Buck Rogers* off the air."

"Why you got your panties in a bunch, dude?" Liam scolded. "Am I wrong?"

A silent pall descended over the basement, each teen with eyes fixed on the floor. A.J. finally broke the quiet.

"You're not wrong. The ghosts could be a side effect of the government's teleportation experiment out at Old Town."

Molly frowned, unconvinced. "Even if the ghosts are a side-effect, I'm not sure the government was behind the glyphs."

A.J. cast a quick glance in Molly's direction, wondering if her statement had something to do with what they saw in the secret building back in June. "You think they were made by actual aliens?"

She shrugged, prying the tab up to open the soda can. "I don't know," she said, raising her can to A.J. "And neither do you."

No one could deny Molly's wisdom in the moment, least of all A.J. She decided to ride this wave for all it was worth. "So Kris, did the ghosts hurt you in any way?"

Taking a moment to reflect on the experience, the boy realized they had not, in fact, caused him any bodily harm. "Uh...I guess not?"

"No," Molly agreed. "They did not. They might be creepy in a *Poltergeist* kinda way, but they're just doing their thing, right?"

The three boys exchanged quick looks, nodding as if in a school lecture.

"So instead of worrying that there are ghosts wandering around town," she proposed, "let's figure out *why* there are ghosts wandering around town. And what it means for the rest of us."

Liam raised both hands from his beanbag in agreement, launching his crumpled soda can at Molly like a free throw from the top of the key on the basketball court. Without blinking or losing a drop of her own soda, she batted the empty can away from her head, banking it into the open wastebasket behind the bar.

"Molly with the assist!" Liam bellowed like a sports commentator.

Although impressed with the athletics of the maneuver, A.J. found himself stuck on the issue of ghosts and the reason for their being suddenly in their lives. "We *do* need to figure out why they're here. I've lived my whole life in this town, and before June I'd never seen a ghost. Why now?"

"Agreed," Molly said.

Kris scratched at an errant itch on his nose. "I guess I can live and let live," he sighed.

A.J. stared at him. "Dude. They're not alive."

Liam saw his opening and dived in head-first, belting out Paul McCartney's Bond theme, *Live and Let Die.*

Eyes rolled and chuckles erupted despite themselves.

"Now," A.J. began, pacing the floor in front of the Atari console on the coffee table, "about the cookies..."

Kris handed out the supply of pumpkin treats he'd brought with him, and ten minutes later, the four teens were on their bikes, scouring the streets from Fourth and Pioneer to First and Cedar, with absolutely zero evidence of ghostly apparitions.

A.J. posited that perhaps there were other conditions they were not privy to, and they returned to Molly's to discuss preparations for Halloween week.

Molly had already assembled a film-worthy replica of Princess Leia's Hoth costume from *The Empire Strikes Back*, while A.J. had decided to go high concept with his Deckard outfit from *Blade Runner*. It consisted of a plaid shirt, knit tie, khakis, and low hiking boots, with a trench coat he'd found at a thrift store in Medford. He procured a suitably large water pistol and sprayed it black, and voila: the spitting image of Harrison Ford's replicant hunter...just fourteen, bespectacled, and pimply.

Liam's *Tron*-themed costume had been a bust. It was essentially a set of white painting coveralls with reflective tape detailing. But the tape kept peeling off in curls, so he decided to keep to his strengths: a closet full of military surplus, and a pressurized water canister, which usually contained weed-killer, but had been thoroughly rinsed and filled with water tinted with orange food coloring. For Liam, who usually dressed in Army surplus anyway, it was "all about the prop". In this case, by adding a combat helmet and the canister in a harness for his back, he was a soldier from the Vietnam War with a flamethrower. The weapon, instead of shooting napalm, shot a stream of orange-tinted water about twenty feet when fully pumped.

Molly thought it looked like pee.

Kris merged creativity with functionality and felt he really nailed the zeitgeist by dressing up as Elliott from *E.T.* The costume had the benefits of being cheap and easily put together, as it consisted merely of a red pullover hoodie and jeans. Not to have his efforts discounted, he did wrap a pillow and a rubber mask of the alien's likeness in a sheet, setting the dummy in the front basket on his bike.

Liam's axiom had turned out to be true: it *was* all about the prop.

The week began quietly, with rallies for Friday's high school football game against, perhaps ironically, the Roseburg Indians. But things took a turn for the worse on Wednesday, when A.J. accidentally walked in on Travis O'Brien and Mick Wulfsohn smoking pot in the locker room between classes.

"Holy shit—it's blink-boy!" O'Brien chuckled.

Mick was suddenly beside him, wrenching his arm behind his back. "Blink out of *this,* blink-boy!"

A tear in the time-space continuum, A.J. thought as the bullies wrestled him against a wall of cold steel locker doors. *I ended up in this space at the wrong time.*

Track 14:
BIG KICK, PLAIN SCRAP

Nick Lowe (1978)

The first punch sent a shock through A.J.'s central nervous system which made him go numb in the face. He tried to curl into a defensive posture, but Mick had him pinned upright to a locker with a forearm across his collarbone.

Crack.

A flash of white exploded in A.J.'s vision and he felt blood rush to his mouth. Lips and gums swelled.

Crack.

Another flash of white and O'Brien's fist drew back, wet with blood. A.J.'s glasses clattered to the ground in two pieces, seemingly miles away.

Thump.

A.J. wheezed as the air left his lungs, his chest seized, and his face became tinged with blue. He fought for breath that didn't come, panic crashing over him in waves. His vision, already blurry, began to collapse from the outside in, a hazy black fog tightening around the periphery.

The assault was over as quickly as it had begun. At the moment A.J.'s body decided the best course of action was to shut down like some prey animals play dead to confuse predators, Bodhi entered the locker room, in mid-conversation with Coach Carlisle.

Jim Carlisle was a former defensive tackle for USC. A knee injury had ended a promising NFL career before it started, which would have provided most people with enough angst for one lifetime, but Carlisle was also a black authority figure in a school full of white kids who liked to push his buttons, and he gave as good as he got.

While the coach pulled O'Brien and Wulfsohn away, one massive hand on the back of each neck, Bodhi went to A.J.'s aid.

The immediate danger passed, A.J.'s lungs finally refilled with air, his vision returned to its slightly blurred normal, and suddenly everything hurt. He slumped down against the lower row of lockers.

"What's this?!" Carlisle demanded. "Something wrong in your head, O'Brien?"

Mick Wulfsohn actually appeared slightly chastened, but O'Brien kept his gaze laser-focused on A.J.

"Nah, Coach. Just a little disagreement."

"Disagreement? What disagreement could you be having that ends up with two seniors attacking a freshman who they outweigh by a hundred pounds combined?"

A.J. winced, both at his throbbing, bloody face, and the accuracy of the statement.

O'Brien didn't even comprehend his own level of hate for A.J. and company. He only knew that he hated them. It was the weird teleporting and how they'd managed to slip his notice all summer. They were associated with things that challenged his reptile brain and he didn't like it. They were *different*. And different wasn't good. Not in rural Oregon teen culture. "Well, you see, that little four-eyed fag thinks he's people..."

The coach bristled at the slur, eyes wide as he tried to maintain his own composure. "That's enough of that talk, O'Brien!" He didn't like Travis. Never had, in fact. The kid was a hellion on the mat, but a liability everywhere else, and now aging out of any usefulness in a high school sports program.

Glancing down, Carlisle saw the gleam of a telescoping aluminum roach clip and the tiny end of a mostly-smoked blunt in its teeth. "Oh, you boys *fully* crapped the bed this time," he warned, plucking the contraband from the cold cement floor and displaying it before the bullies.

For the first time, their collective attention diverted away from their victim.

"That's not mine," O'Brien shrugged, giving Carlisle a punchably-privileged grin.

Mick followed suit. "Never seen it before... what is that, anyway?"

Coach Carlisle wasn't buying what the boys were selling. "I don't care whose it is, but you got the stank all over the both of you." He thrust his chin out, coming almost nose-to-nose with O'Brien. "That's it, boy. That's it for your wrestling career at this school. Take a bow for the people, O'Brien, because you just made a huge dump in your Speedo."

O'Brien made the mistake of meeting Coach Carlisle's gaze. "Won't Principal Evans have something to say about that?"

He immediately regretted it.

"Principal Evans will follow my recommendation, which is that you both be suspended for illegal drug use on school grounds and assaulting a fellow student." He let the words sink in for a moment, then added in a soft, gravelly tone, "And that you both be barred from any sports participation for the rest of the year. Hell, I'd have half a mind to keep you back, but then I'd have to deal with your trailer trash asses for another year." Nodding at Bodhi and his bloody charge, he added, "Better get your pal checked out."

As Carlisle hauled the bullies to the principal's office for disciplinary action, O'Brien leveled a sinister look at A.J.

"This ain't over, you little pussy."

Coach Carlisle shoved them into the hall on their death march to the administration office, admonishing them to "quit that talk", but A.J. instinctively knew O'Brien meant every word, every intent of the implied threat.

"You okay, man?" Bodhi asked, helping A.J. to his feet. "Oh shit, your glasses."

"I'll be okay," A.J. lied, wiping blood from his nose on the sleeve of his sweatshirt. His mouth was swollen and he tasted copper.

Over the summer, the young football star had become much like the older brother A.J. never had. As he gathered up the broken pieces of the freshman's eyeglasses, he laid a gentle arm on his shoulder. "Come on, dude. I'll walk you to the nurse's office."

Nothing was broken. Once his nose stopped bleeding, A.J. was sent home with a split lip, a bandaged gash on the bridge of his nose, and some bruised ribs. A.J. dealt with the assault in the typical way of ignoring his feelings and redirecting his attention to other things. The physical wounds would heal. And he had larger issues to worry about than that waste of DNA, O'Brien.

Instead of their usual pow wow at the diner, Liam and Molly came to hang out at A.J.'s, and Kris brought some food after his shift was done. Liam became visibly angry when A.J. relayed the tale, and Molly promised A.J. a new mix tape to take his mind off the events of the day. Bodhi and Chlöe even made an appearance after football and cheer practice, just to check up on him. The attention was both reassuring and a bit weird, as A.J. wasn't used to being the center of focus in most things. He was much more comfortable observing events at a safe distance.

The trio of Liam, Kris, and A.J. maintained a low profile on Thursday, despite O'Brien and Wulfsohn having been suspended for a week. On Friday, things relaxed a bit. It was Halloween dress-up day at school, and spirit was high going into the Calico-versus-Roseburg football game that afternoon.

Halloween falling on a Sunday that year had put a serious time limit on neighborhood trick-or-treating, although even Molly was starting to consider the activity beneath someone of her age and maturity. The friends decided to attend Friday's football game in costume, then meet at the diner before deciding whose house to commandeer for a weekend of roleplaying games and Atari. It would be Molly's, but the illusion of options was important.

Bodhi threw for 127 yards and four touchdowns, and rushed for another 30 yards on top of that, carrying the Calico High Lumberjacks to victory over the Roseville Indians, 31 to 10. The stellar performance unfortunately ended with a pulled hamstring, and Bodhi went directly home after the game to recuperate, while his friends and teammates went to the diner and the pizzeria to celebrate.

At about 8:10 p.m., the rumors started circulating about O'Brien going to take his dad's car out for the night and finding all four tires deflated. Liam swore on his mother he didn't know who could have done something like that. Regardless, O'Brien and Wulfsohn were now out cruising, with re-inflated tires, looking for A.J. and his crew.

Of course they are, A.J. thought. *It wouldn't be a Friday night in Calico without a credible threat to life and limb—specifically mine.*

While the JV cheer squad took over two booths at the diner, sweaters and miniskirts embellished with matching bunny ears and tails, Grandma Korolewski's pumpkin cookies began circulating among the kids.

It eventually dawned on Kris, Molly, Liam, A.J., and finally Chlöe, that the night was about to get *extremely* weird.

Track 15:
OPEN YOUR EYES
Lords of the New Church (1981)

Chlöe was fifteen, a sophomore who looked like a senior and always seemed composed and perfectly at home no matter where she ventured in the world. Tall and wiry, with a mane of natural blond hair and a shockingly clear complexion, it might be assumed she'd never had an awkward day in her short life. That assumption would have been incorrect. In truth, she had only shed her braces back in May, just after her birthday. She had spent her school years prior in the shadow of Jeannie Wells, as a self-described Jeannie-wannabe, albeit with frizzy hair and acne and poor fashion choices.

Then, over the summer between eighth and ninth grade, The Blossoming occurred. It wasn't just the arrival of curves and clearer skin, but a self-assurance more attractive than any trip to Supercuts could have achieved. She started grooming and dressing better, and boys started to notice. And she noticed them noticing. Chlöe's improved looks rapidly put her in the socialite ranks with Jeannie Wells and her ilk, which could have put her on the path toward shunning her former crowd, but —and this was probably her single most powerfully attractive trait—she was actually a nice person.

She'd offered to go hang out with Bodhi at his house, snuggling on the sofa to watch *The Powers of Matthew Star*, and maybe follow it up with *The Greatest American Hero*. At least the television would be on in the background, adding cover to whatever else might be going on. But Bodhi, already depressed by the sudden end to his celebration, didn't want to transfer those feelings to Chlöe by osmosis. He insisted she go out with her friends on the cheer squad and try to have some fun.

She wasn't having fun.

It wasn't for lack of trying. She put on a brave, happy face and pretended interest in the inane chatter spewing from her more pedestrian cheerleader friends. The entire squad had planned ahead and had donned matching bunny ears and puffy cotton tails with their uniforms in an effort to be provocative. It had earned some disapproving glances from teachers and faculty, but the looks from the zombies and vampires they passed in the halls told them the provocation had worked. Finally, when Molly offered her a pumpkin cookie from the plate being passed among A.J.'s friends, she accepted. That prompted Sibyl to criticize her dietary choices, which drew a round of laughter from Veronica, Stacy, Heather, and Jennifer.

As much as Chlöe was a nice person, neither was she a shrinking violet. Leaning over the table, she made a grand show of shoving the entire cookie into her face, rolling her eyes and mumbling through her stuffed mouth how *amazing* it was, and how they were all missing out on the *best cookies ever*. Then she extended the middle finger on each hand, stepping back to enjoy the shared look of shock across every face in the booth. With a wry smile, Chlöe turned and stormed out of the diner.

The altercation, though not out of the ordinary by small town high school standards, was noticed by A.J.'s group—especially Molly, who had been the cookie instigator.

The four had gathered after the football game, still wearing their costumes from the school day, which meant that Princess Leia and Elliott from *E.T.* were sharing a booth with a Vietnam soldier and a Blade Runner, right across the dining room from the booth full of cheerleader bunnies.

Chlöe was outside the diner for all of thirty seconds before bursting back in, eyes wide. Ignoring the bunnies completely, she strode up to the opposite booth and, grabbing Molly by the hand, hauled her onto her feet and out through the front door.

The three boys exchanged a quick look amongst each other and followed.

"There—do you see it?" Chlöe pointed down 2nd Avenue, toward the intersection with Baker Street. "Oh God, and there's another one!"

Molly gulped and her spine froze like a flagpole in the dead of winter. "Yeah."

The boys assembled behind them, locking in on the object of the girls' attention.

"Ohhhh craaaaap," Kris groaned. "That's... yep."

The ghosts were back, in force. Not merely a half dozen random stragglers, but a veritable parade of the vaporous dead. Natives, pioneers, soldiers, criminals, wealthy matrons, land barons, and saloon girls...those who had died from illness, war, execution, accident or misadventure, appearing much as they had in their last moments of life, but the slightly blurry version one would see in an old photograph. They shimmered luminous and pale in the dark between streetlights, century-old memories given transparent form.

A.J. watched the ethereal pilgrimage work its way south, down Durham toward the First Avenue markets, where the phantoms vanished into the wall of storefronts.

"They're going into the markets," Molly said aloud, giving words to A.J.'s thought process.

"Not *into*," A.J. corrected. "*Through*. I'll bet they're heading to the river."

Chlöe blinked. "You can see them? You can see them!"

"Yeah," A.J. assured her, Molly nodding in solidarity.

"We've seen them before."

"Where...where are they all coming from?" Chlöe mused.

"That's a really good question," A.J. said, looking like a film noir private detective in his trench coat and tie.

Liam scowled. "What the hell? Durham doesn't go to the river. They should be taking Front Street or Cedar."

A series of blank looks from the others told him he'd sort of missed the central point to the whole ghost thing.

"If you'd died a hundred years ago, and didn't have a corporeal body," A.J. posited, "would you bother taking a detour route?"

"And if so," Molly added, "*why?*" With hands on costumed hips, Molly was the spitting image of Princess Leia on the ice planet Hoth.

Chlöe shivered in the autumn breeze. "What are we gonna do? Anything?"

"We're gonna talk to *Babciu*," Kris proclaimed. "She can tell us if anything can be done."

They retreated to the diner and found the elder Mrs. Korolewski in the back of the kitchen, rolling out what had to be her fifteenth batch of pumpkin cookies in a week. She regarded the costumed teens with her white eye and returned to her baking.

"*Babciu*, we need some advice," Kris began. There was an animated exchange in Polish which lasted a solid couple of minutes, the end of which was punctuated by Kris taking a deep breath and sighing awkwardly. "I was afraid of that," he muttered.

If Chlöe was still aware she was wearing her cheerleader uniform and a pair of bunny ears on her head, she hid the knowledge behind a fidgety, excited exterior. "Afraid of what?" she asked, almost manic.

"She says the 'energy is active' tonight," Kris explained. "Something about lines...energy lines."

"Ley lines," A.J. said matter-of-factly. "It's in one of your Time-Life books. The theory is the Earth is covered in them—kind of network of electromagnetic energy."

Kris sighed again. "Well, apparently where the lines meet, you get a...nexus?"

"Yeah?" Liam shrugged. "So?"

"She says that's often where dimensions overlap. It's a good bet that's where they're coming from."

A.J. saw where this was going. "So if we track them back to where they're starting, that's the nexus point. Then what do we do?"

"If it's a doorway to another dimension," Molly interjected, "then we have to close it."

Chlöe's breath caught in her throat, and Liam gave an exaggerated shrug.

"What? Why?" he demanded. "They're not hurting anyone!"

"They can," Kris said seriously.

Silence fell across the kitchen, save for the clank of dishes being washed and Mr. Korolewski doing food prep.

Molly took a step forward. She fully inhabited the character of a princess leading a galactic rebellion, albeit unknowingly. "How?" she asked. "How can they hurt people?"

Kris exchanged a solemn look with his grandmother, who raised a flour-covered hand to make a sign to ward off the Evil Eye before returning to her rolling pin.

"I didn't think she was serious," he said, "but they can take over."

"Take over how?" Molly pressed.

Chlöe, eyes wide, nodded her passive agreement with Molly's line of questioning.

Kris frowned, his brow furrowed as he tried to put the concept into English. "If you're asleep, or drunk, stoned, whatever, she said they just...take over."

"Aw no," Chlöe argued. "No ghost is gonna take over *my* body when I go to sleep."

A.J. wearily raised his hand. "We're gonna seal the nexus," he assured. "We're gonna stop them. Question is, how?"

Liam was about to volunteer the assortment of M80s and other random fireworks on his uniformed person, but the question was already being answered.

"Sea salt and white vinegar," Kris explained. "Something about the chemical makeup neutralizes supernatural energy."

A.J. smacked a fist into his palm and exhaled. "Okay. Squirt guns. Water balloons. We've got to get enough of the stuff up to where these ghosts are coming from. And we need to be able to carry everything on our bikes."

A throat cleared. All eyes turned to Liam, who held his newly-customized garden sprayer/napalm canister. Tapping gently on the metal, he winked at his friends.

"I think I may have just the thing."

Track 16:
SPELLBOUND
Siouxsie & The Banshees (1980)

Twenty minutes later, the supply closet at the diner had been raided and drained of every last two-and-a-half-gallon jug of white vinegar, and Grandmother's hoard of sea salt depleted.

Five friends stood astride their bikes in the parking lot next to the diner, chewing on a fresh batch of pumpkin 'spirit cookies'. Still in costume, their backpacks were laden with a colorful assortment of foul-smelling water balloons. The teens watched silently as a never-ending procession of phantoms hovered down Durham Street toward the markets.

The balloons had come from Liam's backpack, which he called his "bag of holding", but everyone else referred to as his "magic sack of everything", due to its propensity to contain some useful implement when needed. Far from being happenstance, Liam had added the bag of loose balloons at the beginning of October. One never knew when having a ready supply of water balloons might come in handy.

His logic in this regard was often indisputable.

Molly had grown somewhat used to the phantoms, and thought the whole experience was actually pretty cool.

A.J. pocketed the last water balloon that would fit in the coat. He was nowhere near used to seeing ghosts. This totally *wasn't* cool, and never *would* be.

"Gawd, look at them all," Chlöe sighed.

"Okay guys," A.J. instructed. "We're tracking the line to its origin. No side-quests."

Everyone nodded, finding footholds on the pedals of their respective bicycles.

"Oh, and also," Kris added, "O'Brien and Wulfsohn are out looking for us."

A.J. felt the blood drain from his face. "Son of a...thanks for that handy reminder, Kris."

"We'll be okay if we stick together," Liam assured the group, patting the backpack secured to the front handlebars of the Frankenbike. "And I have some...surprises."

They kicked away, out of the diner parking lot and headed north on Union Street, keeping parallel with the ghostly parade on Durham without riding directly into the phantoms. A narrow strip of grass separated Third Avenue from Pioneer Avenue, both of which ran east-west. The open space gave them a decent vantage west to the quaint Deer Park Shopping Center, and east as far as the A&W at Pioneer and Cedar.

The seemingly endless river of spirits continued their walk, the line stretching up past Pioneer, where Durham became Timber Hill Road. Apparently, their ley line nexus was in the middle of an upscale hillside neighborhood.

Despite the chill in the air, downtown Calico was relatively thick with late evening traffic—locals grabbing a quick dinner from Aldo's, or at the burger joint on Pioneer and Main, or parking at the A&W for drive-in tray service. And then there were the late Halloween candy shoppers at Deer Park or the Val-U Drug on Third, behind the diner.

A.J. clenched his teeth and fumed. These people were totally ignorant of the danger they were in, if what Kristof's old Polish grandmother said was true.

As if to illustrate their dire predicament, while A.J. watched, the spirit of a cavalry officer deviated from the parade and disappeared into the body of a sleeping vagrant in front of the apartments across from the bustling A&W.

"Holy shit," Liam exclaimed as they all watched the sleeping man jerk awake and stagger to his feet. "Did you see that?"

It was Elmer Erickson, veteran of the Korean War, a local character with epic stories and an equally epic silver beard. Pushing sixty, the slender veteran resided in an old hunting lodge willed to him by his late brother, but could often be found sleeping outdoors around downtown Calico until winter set in. He wasn't all there, mentally, but he was harmless, and most residents knew him by name.

"Come on," A.J. nodded. "And be ready."

As the group pushed forward on their cycles, Kris finally comprehended the last part of A.J.'s instruction. "Wait...be ready? Be ready for what?"

His question went unanswered. One by one, the gang coasted across Pioneer Avenue, gathering behind Elmer as he shambled toward the collection of people and cars at the A&W.

Despite his trepidation around anything vaguely supernatural, A.J. approached Elmer from the front, waving a halfhearted greeting. "Hey Elmer! How's it g—"

The veteran pushed forward without stopping, and A.J. found himself shoved aside.

Regrouping, A.J. circled around for a second time, taking a position directly in front of the man, creating an effective roadblock. "Hey Elmer. Hold up a second."

Elmer Erickson stopped in his tracks, straightening to face the boy blocking his way. His eyes slowly raised level with A.J.'s, and his bearded mouth pulled back in a tight line over stained, crooked teeth. "Stand aside, you filthy redskin."

It might have been Elmer's voice. A.J. couldn't be sure. He was more focused on the change in the man's facial features. Whether the pumpkin cookies granted him special insight, or whether he'd just known Elmer for years...the man who'd uttered that slur was not Elmer Erickson.

A.J. froze in place, unable to forge a course of action except stammer, "Um...w-what?"

Elmer's eyes widened into saucers, glistening and bloodshot. "I say, stand aside. You damn—"

There was a snapping sound as the water balloon exploded on the back of Elmer's head, showering him with sea salt and vinegar solution. Twitching in response, Elmer hunched forward, hands on knees. A.J. felt a surge of ethereal force barrel into him like a car bumper, knocking him backward to the ground.

Erickson shook his head, blinking, gathering his wits. He spied A.J. on his back, Molly and Kris already at his side to render assistance. Lurching forward and causing Kris to jump, he offered A.J. a gnarled, leathery hand. "You take a stumble, young fella? Here, I'll help ya."

As Elmer, Molly and Kris helped a bewildered A.J. to his feet, Liam shot Chlöe a knowing look.

"There now," Elmer said, as A.J. regained his bearings. "Gotta be careful—sidewalk's a bit uneven out here."

A.J. nodded, realizing Elmer legitimately had no awareness of the last few minutes, that his body had been possessed by the ghost of a U.S. Army officer from the 1800s. "How about you, Elmer—you okay?"

Sniffing at the air suddenly, Elmer perked up. "What the...? Did I piss myself?"

All five teens shrugged in unison.

A.J. fished a five-dollar bill from his wallet and handed it to Erickson. "Here, Elmer. Get yourself a burger."

Elmer brightened. "Well ain't that a kindness! Thank you, young man!"

"After you get some food," Kris advised, "go

home, Elmer."

A.J. nodded in agreement. "Yeah, not safe to sleep on the street tonight."

The group parted ways with the old veteran, who wandered toward the A&W, smelling his worn jacket and trying to discern the source of the wafting acidic odor.

"Dude, did you see that?" Liam marveled, picking up his bike to stand astride the frame.

"See it?" A.J. replied. "I was in its way." He returned to his own bike, Molly and Kris satisfied that he was uninjured.

"Knocked you on your ass," Chlöe added bluntly. "You okay?"

"I think so," A.J. said.

Kris squinted at his friend. "Wonder why it didn't go into you."

A.J. shuddered. The very thought of being possessed by a spirit other than his own sent a chill to every extremity. "Man, don't say that."

Chlöe blinked, clearly having not considered all the ramifications of dealing with ghosts. "W-what? Go into you? They can go into you?"

Liam gave her a blank stare. "Did you *not* just see Elmer get possessed? My hand still reeks from the water balloon I crushed on his head."

Kris seemed heartened by the results of the stealth water balloon assault. "So the stuff works," he muttered proudly. He was about to say something about telling his grandmother, but quickly realized she already knew.

"Maybe," Molly posited, "they can't enter your body if you're awake."

A.J. weighed the thought and decided he might not ever sleep again.

"Or maybe," Liam countered, "they get a whiff of our ghost-banishing gear and are like, 'Zoinks, Scoob!'"

"Possibly," A.J. admitted.

Liam hefted a fresh water balloon from his pack, "You wanna take that chance?"

"What are you—no, wait!"

But before the words had left A.J.'s lips, he felt the latex impact his cheek and the smelled the explosion of vinegar and salt solution over his face and chest.

"Oh, you son of a—"

A sudden flurry of squeals and flailing, close-proximity water balloon launches resulted in all five teens smelling of vinegar and questioning the wisdom of being out that night.

Chlöe was livid. "What...the..."

Liam smiled, vinegar dripping in a slow

rivulet down the side of his nose. "Think of it as a ghost vaccine."

"He's right," A.J. muttered, wiping a vinegar-soaked hand through his already slick hair. "I hate to admit it, but I think this stuff probably neutralizes the spirits, or sends them back to wherever."

"Can you blame them?" Molly grimaced, unable to escape the smell.

Liam flashed a broad grin and made heavy metal horns with his fingers. "Spirit napalm! Righteous!"

Chlöe tensed. "So what if these things start taking over people who are asleep, like the one that possessed Elmer?"

"That's why we have to track them back and shut down the portal," Molly reminded her. "And the sooner the better."

Kris pulled a new pumpkin cookie from his pocket and showed it to the group as a reminder. "And just so we're all on the same timetable, being able to see them..."

They all followed suit, each wolfing down another spiced cookie.

"Okay," A.J. said. "They're coming from somewhere up on Timber Hill. Let's book."

They moved in unison, turning their bikes up Timber Hill Road, as a maroon Oldsmobile Delta 88 angled onto Pioneer.

Track 17:
MYSTERY ACHIEVEMENT
The Pretenders (1980)

The McCabe family were the first millionaires in Oregon. Originally from Colorado mining money, Bertram McCabe had adapted to the Calico recharter by changing his business over to timber, eventually buying stock in several west coast newspapers, and serving a term as mayor. For his residence, McCabe chose a prime lot at the top of Timber Hill, overlooking the entire southwest Rogue River Valley, and there constructed a beautiful, foreboding Victorian home. When the family took possession in April of 1892, it was among the most palatial dwellings in the Pacific Northwest, complete with geometric turrets, imported oak staircases, leaded glass windows, and ornate gingerbread trim. It was painted a bright shade of orchid with brick red and cream accents, trimmed in white.

Bertram McCabe was the epitome of the old adage "burning the midnight oil", the warm kerosene lamplight from his study windows peering down at the community like a vigilant guardian.

But the home's amber eyes only gazed over the town for a period of twenty years. An outbreak of typhoid fever swept through the Rogue River in the summer of 1912, wiping out the three generations of McCabes who lived in the house. Although buried a short distance away in the cemetery off Corvus Road, no extended family emerged to take possession of the estate, and the colossal Victorian had stood, empty and dark, ever since.

Now leaky and wind-worn, its gables rotting and windows broken, the old house had become a place for teen mischief and initiations, much like Old Town Calico. But whereas Old Town was easily patrolled by the Curry County Sheriff's Department due to its accessible location off the North Bank road, the McCabe house stood atop a hill, at the end of a spiraling residential street, and was surrounded by a massive wrought iron fence and greenery growing unchecked.

In three quarters of a century, the McCabe mansion had become a cliché—a dark leviathan atop a lonely hill, the quintessential "haunted house" out of Central Casting.

Fully charged with Grandmother's spirit cookies and reeking of vinegar, the five teens pumped their bikes on the incline of Timber Hill Road, the grade growing ever steeper with every several yards pedaled. The phantoms passed them in their constant parade, shimmering as they drifted by, oblivious of the kids traveling against both the ethereal tide and gravity itself.

As they negotiated the spiral curve, approaching the spur of Yearling Road which branched off toward an upscale community of more modern hillside homes, A.J. saw a flash of car headlights paint the trees to their right in a white glare. "Oh shit," he mumbled aloud. "Come on! Off the road!"

Leading the group to the left, toward the hill's interior, A.J. zipped off the street and into a labyrinth of rocks and bushes. The four others followed, skittering to a halt on the dirt trail, out of sight of the rumbling muscle car as it ascended slowly, eventually passing them on its trek toward the hilltop mansion.

Liam was the first to identify the car. "Shit," he whispered. "It's O'Brien."

A.J. shivered despite his costume's trench coat. "Aww, what the hell, man?"

"I don't think they saw us," Liam asserted, squinting out past the bushes.

"What do you wanna do, chief?" Molly asked. "Come back another time?"

A.J. gave her a soft look and shook his head. "Absolutely not," he replied. "We're doing this once. One time only. Not gonna let O'Brien get into my head."

Kris nodded in agreement. "Especially when there's enough *ghosts* to get into your head."

A.J. shivered again. "Not helping, Kris!"

Chlöe leaned forward on her handlebars, still astride her bike. "So are we gonna wait for O'Brien to get tired of looking for us and then finish riding up?"

A.J. had a different plan, and was already leaning his bike over in some brush against the hillside. "Ditch the bikes," he said. "We go on foot. The trail winds up the hill to the Mc-Cabe property. We should be able to get onto the grounds from the back."

"What if we get up there and O'Brien is *also* up there?" Chlöe worried.

"We'll burn that bridge when we get there," A.J. replied, heading up the steep trail.

Molly wasn't sure if the mixed metaphor was intentional or not, but she went with it, leaning her bike over next to A.J.'s and following him up the footway into the dark.

A couple of lonely flashlight beams probed the dirt path as it wound up the side of Timber Hill, zig-zagging back and forth to create a gentler incline than the overall grade. A few minutes later, the trail leveled out in some evergreens and the party found itself at the fence tracing the outer perimeter of the McCabe property. A black cage of bars, capped with decorative spear points, traveled north-south along the outer length of the grounds, cutting east-west at the upper and lower corners. It was perhaps eight feet in height, not including the points, the bars spaced so that only Molly could squeeze through.

She had to remove the quilted Princess Leia vest, but once through, she was able to take custody of the backpacks as the others passed them between the bars, preparing for a hazardous climb over. The vest itself was flung over the sharp points atop the fence, creating a makeshift cushion against impalement.

Liam grabbed hold of a bar and was about to shimmy up when Kris noted the weld at the top was rusted almost through. The four on the outside scanned the attachment points along the top and bottom rails, and found that many of the welds were decayed to the point of collapse. Within moments, Liam had kicked down a few bars with his combat boots, creating an easy passage into the property.

They found themselves in the back forty, in the cover of some overgrown maples. Ferns and brush sprouted from a patchy, moss-covered lawn. The McCabe mansion towered into the moonlit sky perhaps forty paces distant, its dark silhouette ominous and imposing.

A.J. turned to the group when all were through the perimeter. "You guys hold up here for a sec," he instructed. "Let me go around and scope out the front." He slung his backpack to the ground and unzipped it, producing a water balloon from within. As he carefully stashed it in the pocket of his trench coat, Molly stepped forward, shrugging back into her Princess Leia vest.

"I'm going with you."

"No need, Molly. I'll be right back."

Without looking at him, Molly opened the stopper at the back of her squirt gun and shook it slightly to check the fluid level inside. "I don't think you heard me."

Kris and Chlöe exchanged a look with each other, then with Liam. All three shrugged.

"What are you looking for?" Chlöe asked.

A.J.'s lips pursed into a U-shape. "I want to see where the phantoms are leaving the house, and if O'Brien and Wulfsohn are hanging out anywhere."

Liam hefted his Maglite in a dirty hand. "We'll watch for your light. Hit your beam—one long for go, two short for stop."

"And if you guys hear screaming," Molly added, "come pitch in, huh?"

Then she was away, heading for the side of the giant house at a jog, leaving A.J. to catch up. It was only a short jaunt, but the night was dark and neither one of them had a flashlight on, for fear of being seen.

The two rounded the front corner of the mansion's footprint, able to make out the east end of its wraparound porch. The columns flaked century-old paint. Gables and siding hung warped and spotted with mold and algae.

The oak front door tilted open, missing a hinge, the fan-light in its upper quadrant shattered and hollow. As Molly and A.J. watched from a safe distance, the procession of ghosts continued, shimmering phantoms hovering out through the doorway and down the path to the front gate. The gate itself hung open in partial collapse, creating an opening for the ghosts to float through into the wide world outside.

"God, look at them," Molly sighed.

A.J. squinted through his glasses. "We have to stop this."

"We're gonna close the nexus as soon as we...go in," Molly gulped, suddenly conscious of the task ahead.

"I know," A.J. said. "But how many have already escaped? How many more will escape before we get it closed?"

Molly blinked, a sudden brainstorm upon her. "Hey, remember those books Kris has?"

"Yeah? What about 'em?"

Molly thought back to the volume on ghosts and spirits, recalling a passage she'd found interesting. "One of the things people used to do to keep spirits away was put iron across the threshold of a doorway..."

A.J. was already in sync with her thought process. "Stay here," he said. "I'll be right back."

He was gone in an instant, and returned moments later with the rest of the gang in tow. Each held at least one broken fence rod.

"We're going in the front door," A.J. said. "And we're gonna lay one of these across every exterior doorway we find."

Liam scanned the night toward the residential road to the south. "Any sign of O'Brien?"

"Not so far," Molly answered.

Chlöe fidgeted nervously with her iron bar. "Hey guys, if we're gonna do this, let's just do it."

A.J. found each of his friends' faces in the dark. Kris was easy to see, having gone pale. Everyone nodded in unison.

"Let's go," he said, with more authority than he felt worthy of.

Bracing themselves against an ever-flowing ethereal tide, the five friends scuttled forward with squirt guns, water balloons and iron rods. Rick Deckard and Princess Leia, the cheerleader bunny, Elliott, and the Vietnam soldier.

A.J. dropped his iron bar across the front door threshold as he stepped past the hanging door. Immediately, the phantoms roaming the old house began searching for a different mode of egress. Individual spirits backed up in a bizarre queue, and some took notice of the incursion of flesh and blood. The other four followed him in, watching as a gauzy blue-white river of souls crowded into the entry hall, spreading into the space with confused, angry looks on transparent faces.

Kris had never been so simultaneously glad and yet resentful of his grandmother's cooking.

Liam flicked on his Maglite and ran the beam up the oak staircase to the second floor, and Molly slapped the back of his head.

"No," she scolded. "No stairs."

"Lay the bars across the bottom of every exterior doorway," A.J. instructed. "There's one at the end of this hallway, one in the kitchen and one in the ballroom."

Nobody was all that surprised that A.J. knew the layout of the McCabe mansion as if he were reading from the blueprints in front of them. Silently they split into two groups: Laim, Chlöe, and Kris headed to the rear of the house with iron bars and flashlights to secure the back and kitchen doors, while A.J. and Molly worked their way toward the source of the spiritual parade. It looked as though the entire procession began in the ground floor ballroom, and Molly had a bar intended for the exterior door.

On the road outside, the maroon Oldsmobile sat dark, its headlights off. A brief glint of moonlight reflected off the bottle of Olympia beer as Travis O'Brien took a swig, watching the play of a single flashlight within the old house. Mick Wulfsohn followed in turn, gulping from an identical glass bottle.

"Check it out," O'Brien muttered in a low tone. "Looks like the *Scooby Doo* gang is back."

Mick was already tipsy, but he held his expression like a granite mask. "Little shits."

"You ready?" O'Brien asked, his eyes riveted on the front of the mansion.

Mick hesitated. "Ready for what?"

"Ready for a little fun..."

Track 18:
SATURDAY NIGHT IN THE CITY OF THE DEAD
Ultravox (1977)

"Nah, man, I'm good," Mick declined, trying to remember how many empty beer bottles now littered the back seat floor.

But O'Brien had already flung open the driver's side door and was stalking toward the house in his faded Levi's and sleeveless flannel shirt. "Suit your damn self," he mumbled, his cheeks flushing red. These punks would get a proper ass-whupping tonight. All of 'em. Even without Mick's help.

Screw Wulfsohn, O'Brien thought. *That's right, I'll take all of those little shits myself if I have to.*

Before he knew it, his feet were carrying his muscled frame at an unintended dead run. There was a brief moment of elation as he cleared the front steps and sailed through the entry, past the broken door, then a twinge of panic as his foot plunged through a rotting floorboard, and finally blackness as his head collided with the stairway banister.

CR

A.J.'s group had just arrived in what a century ago had been a formal ballroom, although the number of formal dance parties actually held here could have been counted on one hand. Its once-polished parquet floors now buckled into tiny mountain ranges across its length, and the tarnished brass chandelier that once hung from the middle of the ceiling now lay on its side in the corner. At the room's center, a rippling, pulsating rift in space hovered in the air before them, crackling with tendrils of static electricity. Every couple of seconds, like a revolving door, a ghostly traveler would emerge, joining the line to exit the house and be released into the world outside. If the nexus was a gateway between dimensions, the house was a clearly staging ground, a way station of sorts.

The five teens stood agape, eclectic Halloween costumes somehow appropriate, given the variety of fashion worn by their ethereal counterparts. Like they'd seen on the streets of Calico, the disembodied spirits of dead settlers, natives, miners, and rogues filled the room, as if waiting for the band to play a waltz.

The ghostly pale light at the center of the nexus was bright enough that Liam pulled his aviators from the inside pocket of the Army jacket, placing the mirrored frames over his straining eyes.

Kris heard the crash behind them and turned back toward the entry hall. "What was that?"

A.J. pulled the water balloon from his pocket and felt it wobble in his palm. "Never mind, Kris," he croaked. "Let's get this done."

The balloon arced through the air, coming down in the center of the ballroom floor, where the ley line nexus pulsed and expanded like an alien heart. It split on impact, spraying its contents of sea salt and vinegar in a small radius. The rift shimmered and contracted, almost as if in pain. An inhuman groan echoed throughout the cavernous room.

Immediately, every wandering spirit turned its attention toward the five teens, crowding around their position in the wide double doorway. Just as suddenly, the room erupted in an all-out water balloon and squirt gun assault.

The phantasms, having initially given the kids a wide berth due to their salt and vinegar inoculations, began reaching out in some voiceless instinct to stop their efforts. Molly's index finger was as rapid-fire on her water gun's trigger as it was on the Atari fire button at home. As bursts of alchemical solution spit from the barrel of her weapon, the apparitions cried out silently as if wounded by real bullets, their transparent forms rending apart and dissipating into nothingness.

"Liam!" A.J. hailed, tossing a second balloon into the rift and firing his painted squirt gun at the face of a ghostly prospector. "Napalm the nexus!"

Without a second thought, Liam scurried to the rear of the massive room, whipping the garden canister in front of him on the arm strap. Grabbing the pump handle in his left hand, he began pressurizing the contents.

Kris and Chlöe moved out of the hallway and into the room, letting loose with a barrage of water balloons from their backpacks. Several splattered across the floor against the exterior walls, passing through the spirits aimed at. They recalibrated, turning their primary focus toward the nexus, which now oscillated at a frequency like a sonic vibration across the surface of water. Each new payload of sea salt and vinegar washed into the rift and caused a convulsion, almost like a wave of nausea.

Suddenly Liam stood, aiming the pressure wand in front of him, letting loose a spray of the mystical solution in the canister. Shimmering blue-white light sent caustics across the walls and ceiling. The house echoed with unearthly moans, the ballroom floor warping around the hole in time and space.

"That's doing it!" A.J. cried, hopeful for the first time tonight.

Then something knocked into Kris from behind, and the boy went sprawling to the buckled floor. Chlöe followed, collapsing to a heap with a giant welt on her bare leg.

A.J. and Molly turned to look.

O'Brien—or whatever was possessing him—stood in the doorway, wide of stance and clutching one of the turned spindles from the staircase like a club. His head was lowered but he gazed up defiantly, a sinister grin slowly creeping across his broad face.

Liam kept his attention and the gardening wand on the rift opening, pumping the canister as he sprayed the solution into the center of the nexus. The abstract sounds of discomfort now bled into the very bones of the house, seeming to emanate from every wall, every door, every ceiling joist. The ethereal portal contracted and shuddered again and again, decreasing in diameter each time.

O'Brien shifted his gaze, and he met eyes with A.J., who knew in in instant that it was not really him, but some possessing spirit. The bully's arm cocked back to strike with his makeshift weapon, A.J. temporarily frozen in terror.

Molly's arm rocketed out, hurling a purple water balloon with pinpoint accuracy. The tiny latex bomb exploded on impact with O'Brien's jaw, sending an explosion of aromatic liquid across his face and chest, soaking his tank top and plaid flannel.

O'Brien doubled over as if kicked in the stomach, the ethereal form of his possessing spirit careening out the back of him and escaping away into the entry hall. His physical form crumpled in a heap to the floor, slamming his head again.

As Kris and Chlöe staggered back to their feet, content that O'Brien was unconscious, A.J. and Molly turned to look at the nexus. The portal had decreased by more than half in size and apparent volume. Trading a look and a nod, each took what water balloons remained and began a machine gun purification of the nexus.

Splat after satisfying *splat* sent Grandmother's ethereal neutralizing fluid into the interdimensional gateway. Each impact caused the warping portal to pulse and shrink, scream and vibrate through the old mansion.

"It's closing!" Liam reported from across the room. "We're doing it!"

Chlöe and Kris continued lobbing balloons until their packs were empty. A.J. and Molly turned their attention back toward the wandering spirits in their midst, gunning down the last few of them with squirt guns and some choice profanity.

There was a sudden thunderclap of air rushing to fill a void, and the rift shrank in on itself and was torn from existence, a faint smell of ozone hanging in the air.

A.J. and Liam examined the ballroom floor where the rift had been. It was soaked in vinegar, but otherwise no different than before the ley line nexus had opened.

The friends took turns exchanging knowing glances before A.J. muttered, "Let's get the hell out of here," and they stumbled toward the front door.

∞

From the front seat of the Delta, Mick Wulfsohn watched the Calico Kids take a hard left at the front corner of the porch and disappear into the trees at the back of the property. Immediately concerned for O'Brien's fate, he tossed his fifth beer bottle into the back seat and slid across the front to exit the open driver's side.

In doing so, his hand slipped from the steering wheel, jacket sleeve pulling the gear shifter to Neutral. As Mick Wulfsohn went to render aid to his unconscious friend inside the McCabe mansion, O'Brien's father's Oldsmobile slowly rolled backward down Timber Hill Road.

Track 19:
BLIND YOUTH
The Human League (1978)

Five bikes split off from each other at Fourth and Baker, heading in five different directions. By 2 a.m., the riders had made it home.

The town grapevine sprouted to life early Saturday morning with news of the strange happenings at the McCabe house. Sheriff Chavez had been called to the scene by an anonymous report of a loud crash and shouting on the property, a sure indication that teenage shenanigans of one kind or another were afoot. What she found was two inebriated males, and a maroon Olds Delta 88 sitting nose-up in a ditch just beyond the curve in Timber Hill Road.

Deputy Halverson poked around inside, discovering an assortment of colorful latex shreds on the floor of the ballroom, along with a spindle taken from the staircase handrail. There was no other evidence of vandalism, but the whole place smelled like an outhouse.

Mick Wulfsohn claimed to have discovered Travis O'Brien inside the mansion with a couple of swollen goose-eggs on either side of his head, and no idea as to how the Olds had rolled backwards over six hundred feet into the drainage ditch. O'Brien went on and on about "Goddamn ghosts everywhere", but otherwise had no explanation for why he'd been inside the abandoned house. Neither one claimed to know where the empty beer bottles in the Delta's backseat had come from.

Halverson noted that O'Brien reeked of vinegar and Oly beer.

Both boys were taken home and remanded to parental custody, and a tow truck was dispatched from Gold Beach to fish the car out of the gully.

A.J. put a call out to the gang, and by 3 p.m. a meeting had convened in Molly's rec room to discuss the events of the previous night. Liam called it a "post-mortem", much to A.J.'s disgust, although he had to admit the term was apt. He also would have preferred an earlier rendezvous, but Kris had been on the Saturday breakfast and lunch schedule at the diner.

He was greeted with a loud "Where the hell have you been?" from Liam when he finally arrived at 3:20, but Molly tossed him a can of Rondo from the mini fridge, and all was right with the world.

A.J. had his nose buried in a library book on geomancy, while Chlöe and Bodhi took turns playing Space Invaders on the Atari. Liam and Molly appeared to have a halfhearted pool game underway.

"Sorry," Kris explained, popping open the soda can. "I had to give *Babciu* a full report. Jesus, those cookies."

Molly nodded, returning to her pool cue and setting up a tricky bank shot. "Amen to that. I'm so sick of pumpkin."

"My dad wants to start selling them, like all over," Kris reported, "but mom doesn't think there's a market for pumpkin spice anything."

Liam chuckled at the very notion. "I gotta agree with your mom, dude. But what does Grandma say?"

"Nothing," Kris shrugged, leaning against the wet bar and swigging from the cold can. "She just winked at me. Not sure if she understands what we did or if she was having a stroke."

"And what exactly did you guys do?" Bodhi asked, setting his game controller on the coffee table and turning to face the majority of the group.

"Aside from knocking a ghost out of Travis O'Brien?" Chlöe offered.

Liam flashed a grin in her direction. "That was so cool."

A.J. closed his reference book with a *thump* and looked up from his beanbag seat. "Pretty sure we closed a ley line nexus, and figured out why there's so much unexplained phenomena around here."

Bodhi blinked and shook a head of feathered blond hair. "Okay, Brainiac. Once more, in English."

A.J. rolled out of the beanbag and stood up, heading to the mini fridge. "You know how the Force is this invisible energy field that binds the galaxy together?"

"Now you're speaking my language," Bodhi quipped, raising his own Pepsi as A.J. produced a can of root beer and shut the fridge door.

"Well, pretend that the Force is a real thing, and that energy crisscrosses all over the planet. And places where enough of these meridians cross each other, you get what's called a *nexus*, where it's possible to open a rift into an alternate dimension..."

Chlöe stared at A.J. without blinking. "Is that where the phantoms come from?"

"Don't see why not," A.J. replied with a quick shrug, pounding a gulp of root beer and punctuating with a resonant belch. "We exist in *this* dimension, they exist in *theirs*, and the rift allowed them to cross over into *ours*."

"What about the ghosts we saw out at Old Town?" Molly posed, a furrow creeping across her brow. "Was there another nexus somewhere out there? Was that what made the teleportation happen?"

A.J. leaned against the counter next to Kris. He wasn't altogether comfortable being the center of attention and holding court like this, but in a strange way it felt natural to be sharing his theories on parallel universes with his closest friends. Molly's basement rec room was a safe place. Nobody here would beat him up for being weird. "It would make sense," he began, "that there was some kind of breach in the membrane between dimensions—"

Chlöe screwed up her face in revulsion. "*Membrane?* Eww!"

"Dude, you could just say 'wall' or 'curtain'," Kris suggested quietly.

A.J.'s eyes rolled back in his head and he let out an exhausted sigh. "It wouldn't be accurate. You were there last night. We were all there—except Bodhi—and we saw it. It's like a living thing."

"Like in *Poltergeist*," Liam gestured with his pool cue. "When they pulled Diane and Carol Anne through the ceiling..."

Chlöe shuddered. "That...was...so gross!"

"Dude, it was rad!" Liam insisted.

Molly chuckled. "It was pretty gnarly."

"Definitely *moist*," Bodhi nodded, knowing how much Chlöe detested the word.

"Ugh, 'moist'? Really?" Chlöe gasped, incredulous. "You know I hate that."

"What?" Bodhi frowned, shrugging innocently. "Moist?"

The group erupted in agreement that the movie sequence in question was indeed *moist*, which earned Bodhi a slug in the right shoulder.

"Ow!" he protested theatrically. "Throwing arm!"

Realizing what she'd done, Chlöe winced and began softly rubbing the point of impact on his outer bicep, apologizing through clenched teeth.

Bodhi couldn't help the devious grin that broke across his face. "So anyway," he said, turning back to A.J., "breach in the membrane..."

Chlöe leaned back, regarding Bodhi with a murderous side-eye. She pushed away from her boyfriend, standing to grab a refreshment from the fridge. "Nice," she hissed through a smirk dripping with sarcasm.

"It would follow," A.J. said, trying to ignore the lovers' spat unfolding before them, "that there's a ley line running north-south through Old Town, since that's the path we saw the original ghosts on."

"What if that's how the teleportation works?" Molly said, more to herself than to A.J.

"We don't know exactly what makes it work," A.J. stated. "If it's a living system, it's probably attuned to other biological life energy."

"Dude," Kris blinked. "What if that's what sank Old Calico?"

Liam let the butt of his cue stick hit the ground. "Where did they execute those Indians?"

A.J. was already ahead of him. "North side of town. Up by the mines."

"So a bunch of life force basically dumped on a ley line," Molly added. "Like lighter fluid on a campfire."

"*Fwoosh*," A.J. nodded.

Liam joined him. "The mine explosions, the sinkholes, all in that north-south line down Main Street."

"Holy shit, you guys," Bodhi marveled. "Well done. This is some next-level Kolchak stuff right here."

Chlöe popped the tab on her soda. "You mean *Kojak*."

"You're so pretty," Bodhi sighed. "*Kolchak —the Night Stalker*."

Liam flashed a grin. "Darren McGavin as a ghost-hunting reporter! Dude, I loved that show!"

"Everyone would have known *Scooby Doo*," Chlöe argued. "You could have just said that."

"Except," A.J. countered, "this is like capturing the creep, pulling off the rubber mask, and finding a scarier creep instead of Old Man Jenkins."

Bodhi was suddenly interested beyond the casual lark of it all. "What do you mean?"

"It's bad enough that the pioneers who founded the original town murdered a bunch of innocent natives and caused the disaster that forced the town to move." A.J. began to pace the floor aimlessly, eyes downcast. "But now we've got a government agency doing experiments in teleportation along the same ley lines. Which means they're working with the same concept of geomancy."

"Yeah, but we're not going back there," Liam insisted. "We're in the clear."

"I don't know if we'll ever truly be in the clear," A.J. stated dryly, and a pall descended over the party atmosphere in the rec room. "Kris, you remember the book report we did in History class in seventh grade?"

"In Thurston's class?" Kris confirmed. "Um, I think so?"

A.J. cracked open the reference book on the bar counter to where a piece of folded binder paper marked its place. "The Shasta war band leader executed in Calico."

Kris was perplexed. He glanced at the ceiling, and finally recalled. "Black Eagle."

A.J. unfolded the sheet of paper to reveal the sketch he'd made of the logo he and Molly had seen inside the installation.

A stylized black eagle.

"Oh my *gawd*," Molly whispered.

A long and profound silence fell over the group. Nobody spoke for an eternity.

Suddenly Liam slapped the pool rack on the table and the sound jarred everyone from their stupor.

"Come on, people," he said. "It's not like we can actually *do* anything about it. Just keep our heads down and quit getting involved in things that include ley lines, dimensional portals, and government teleportation experiments."

"Hey, we did the community a service!" Kris protested.

Liam rearranged the stripes and solids so that the 8-ball sat in the middle of the rack before pulling it away. "Yeah, we seem to be doing a lot of that lately. At least we got a reward for finding Jeannie and Eric."

"They can't know," Molly said.

"Nobody can know," A.J. agreed. "We did it for us, as well as the town. Not everything has to have a reward, aside from *we get to live*."

"So the plan is to do nothing," Chlöe affirmed, finally taking a long pull from her can of Pepsi.

A.J. glanced over his left shoulder at her and nodded. "Exactly. Keep our heads down and stay off the radar of the Sheriff's Department."

"I can do nothing," Molly affirmed.

Kris offered his can of Rondo in a toast. "To nothing."

"Nothing," Bodhi repeated.

Liam leaned over the pool table, extending his cue for the break. "Amen," he said, sending the white cue ball smacking into the grouping at the opposite end of the table. "To nothing."

Track 20:
A FOREST
The Cure (1980)

Doing nothing sounded good in theory, and for the next month, the group was true to its word. November came and went. The maples, alders, and dogwoods went from a vibrant tapestry of red and gold to sparse, skeletal fingers grasping toward the sky. The coniferous majority stood by, unchanged and unmoved.

Travis O'Brien was neither seen nor heard from all month. His expulsion and later "incident" at the McCabe house had a chastening effect on Mick Wulfsohn, who kept his head down and gave A.J. and his friends a wide berth.

This made school downright tolerable. Not fun by any means, but tolerable.

The diner shut down for Thanksgiving, and the Korolewskis said blessings over a modest family feast, the real star of which was Grandmother's pumpkin pie. She assured Kris that it was not "special like the cookies", but he declined just the same.

Molly's household put out a decent spread. The commercial real estate biz had been good this year. She and Bodhi made each other laugh across the table, until both parents had suffered enough and sent them down to the rec room to play Atari.

A.J. shared a small feast of turkey, mashed potatoes, and green bean casserole with his parents, then snoozed on the sofa next to his dad while they watched the New York Giants beat the Detroit Lions on television.

Fellow football spectators included Liam and his mother, albeit over Hungry Man dinners on TV trays in the living room.

It surprised no one that during the first week in December news arrived through the high school grapevine that O'Brien had joined the Marines and was shipping out for Camp Pendleton. A.J. thought perhaps giving O'Brien a gun and teaching him how to kill people was probably not the best idea, but Liam reassured him that the Corps would break him down and remake his personality from scratch. And the new personality couldn't possibly be worse than the original one. Right?

Thinking perhaps he'd dodged one last fig-urative bullet from O'Brien, A.J.'s stomach sank into his legs when he literally bumped into the human sparkplug coming out of the Val-U Drug on 3rd. A.J.'s purchase of graph paper and pencils for map-making skittered onto the sidewalk, and he braced for punches that never landed.

"Oh, sorry, dude." O'Brien stooped over, picking up the ream of paper and the box of Ticonderoga Number Twos. He stood, offering the items with his gap-toothed smile, his mas-sive bulk dwarfing A.J.'s skinny frame despite being almost matched in height. As A.J. ac-cepted the gesture with a nod and a quiet "Thank you", he met O'Brien's eyes and came to a startling realization.

There was no recognition in his gaze. He didn't remember.

Just *who* and *how much* he didn't remem-ber, A.J. couldn't be sure. But he wasn't about to test the boundaries. He'd only just gotten his glasses replaced after the pre-Halloween beating at school. Shoving his purchase into his backpack, he saddled up on his bike and pedaled away, unaware that was the last time he would see O'Brien. At least for a very long while.

In coastal Oregon, December usually meant rain, but 1982 proved to be skimpy with precipitation. By the third week, the schools were on winter break, and families packed for holiday ski trips or just settled in for the arrival of 1983.

Bodhi decided to spend Christmas in LA with some childhood friends, and the rest of A.J.'s group all but moved into Molly's basement, the gang having begun what A.J. thought was probably his most ambitious *D&D* campaign ever.

This hazy, late Sunday morning, as two pizza boxes sat open on the pool table, A.J., Molly, Kris, Liam, and Chlöe gathered on the floor around the coffee table to stuff their gobs with cheese and pepperoni, and thrill to the adventure at hand.

Kris and Liam were neck deep in a debate over the advantages of the longbow over mounted cavalry, and whether the Battle of Agincourt was really a valid indicator of supremacy, or if weather and mud had more to do with the French defeat—

The lights flickered and went dark a moment before the sonic boom reached the house.

"What was that?" Chlöe worried, glancing around the rec room for answers that weren't forthcoming.

Kris leaped to his feet. "Russians?"

"Oh thank gawd," Molly sighed.

"It's not the Russians, you dork." Liam stood casually, ambling to the daylight basement window that overlooked the hillside, the river, and the south bank beyond.

The others followed suit, a mass of faces crowding around the rectangular glass pane. Another seeming clap of thunder exploded directly overhead, and the window was suddenly filled with light and heat. The rocketing object was round and flat, the shape of a waffle iron, fifty feet across, trailing streamers of fire and smoke. It descended across the river, shooting toward the wetlands and forest beyond.

As they watched, the meteor—or flying saucer, or whatever it was—skimmed the tree line near the Siskyou National Forest before disappearing. They saw the orange flicker from an explosion seconds before the sound reached them, along with a shockwave that caused every surface in the house to vibrate.

A collective gasp erupted from the faces crowded at the window, creating tiny individual fog rings on the glass.

Liam swallowed. "Whoa."

A.J. and Kris exchanged a look and simultaneously asked, "Did you feel that?"

"What...what do you think it is? Er...*was*." Chlöe paraphrased her earlier question, unsatisfied with the notion of a Russian invasion or nuclear attack. Whatever had just crashed in the forest between Calico and Gold Beach hadn't looked like a Soviet rocket, and the explosion had been distinctly un-mushroom-shaped.

A.J. shrugged, still staring out the fogged window. "Meteor, probably. No way to be sure, without—"

"—without going out there," Molly finished. Her eyes brightened with the smile of abject mischief creeping across her face. "I just can't stand not knowing," she said. "Can you?"

A.J. returned the look with eyes wide in a nervous warning. "Oh, no. Really?"

Liam was all in, grabbing a couple of cans of root beer from the mini fridge, and stashing them in his backpack. "You weenies coming, or you staying here to finger-paint with your drool?"

A.J. cleared his throat, but it did nothing to rid his voice of the adolescent squeak that came out with his next sentence. "Uh...guys? I thought we were gonna practice Zen and the art of doing nothing?"

Before he knew what was happening, the streets of Calico were whizzing by under his bike pedals, as the pack of friends made their way to the North Bank road. Unable to simply cross the Rogue at the downtown shore, they were posed with a dilemma: either head west to the Wedderburn Bridge and proceed through Gold Beach; or wind their way east, past Old Town Calico and into the Siskiyou National Forest. Once beyond the forest border, it was less than a mile to the Lobster Creek Bridge to Jerry Flat Road, which ran along the south bank of the Rogue.

Another mile put them back outside federal lands, among a patchwork of wetlands, motorcycle trails and scattered groves of evergreens. A thick mist lay like a down comforter over the river tributaries and small fishing lakes.

Liam led the convoy. He knew this area best, although A.J. and Kris had joined him fishing on several occasions. They followed the rising column of smoke to a hillside just beyond the finger of an old timber access that ran back toward Gold Beach, ditching their bikes at the foot of the wooded hill, and creeping quietly toward the top.

Sheriff Chavez and Deputy Halverson were both already on the scene, their Broncos parked at a safe distance from the considerable trough through the forest floor. Whatever had made the impressive channel remained hidden at the far end, but the furrow itself was at least a hundred feet long and twenty wide, and the impact had torn entire trees from the soil, flinging them randomly like pick-up sticks.

A.J. tried to flag Liam's attention to figure out how to get to the final resting place of the object without being seen by Curry County's finest, but his eyes were drawn back to the impact site, where a black Chevy Suburban was just sliding to a gravelly halt on the trail.

A.J. and Molly found each other's gaze, and their eyes widened in unison.

The vehicle door bore the Black Eagle insignia.

Track 21:
LOOKING FOR CLUES
Robert Palmer (1979)

Over the next hour, as the five friends lay on their bellies in the soft carpet of pine needles and moss, traffic at the impact site increased exponentially. First came a rust-red pickup bearing a middle-aged hunter with a matching pair of Bluetick Coonhounds and a tagged black bear carcass in the bed. He'd been breaking down his hunting camp about five miles away when the impact had spooked his dogs.

Not five minutes later, a science team from the University of Oregon arrived in a panel van, clad in hazmat suits and armed with Geiger counters. Then the Forestry Service showed up, followed by an Oregon State Trooper in a prowler that would have been chasing down speeders on Highway 101 outside Port Orford, had he not seen the meteor's arrival and rushed to investigate. A few Gold

Beach locals, river tourists, and National Park rangers arrived to gawk and snap a few photos with their Polaroids and pocket Instamatics.

Sheriff Chavez successfully kept most of the visitors at bay, allowing uniformed officials and grad students to have a look and take their readings, but eventually the black-suited man and woman who'd come in the Suburban tired of the spectacle and started flashing their federal badges around. The spectators gradually dispersed, and the federal agents disappeared into the woods toward the meteorite's resting place, leaving Chavez to deal with the kids on the hill.

"I know you're up there," she announced from about twenty feet beyond Liam's hiding spot. "Nothing here of interest."

A.J. thought of the federal agents, screwed up all his courage and, without revealing himself from the fallen tree trunk, replied: "We beg to differ."

Chavez allowed the hint of a smile. She liked these kids. Hell, if she were fourteen, she would have been hanging out with them. "Beg all you want," she said. "You need to run along now, or explain to your parents why you're sitting in a holding cell in the Curry County Jail. If you try to draw this out, or make us come up there, it'll just go worse for you."

Five faces exchanged looks of profound frustration, and Liam sighed.

"Solid point, Sheriff." He shot A.J. a glance, and was met with a nod toward the forest, where the meteor had come to a stop.

"Don't try circling back around on me," Chavez warned. "Deputy Halverson is down at the crater, and he'd love nothing more than to sit you in jail all night."

A.J. rolled his eyes. She really was playing three-dimensional chess most of the time.

Liam scanned the impact site from behind his fallen log, and saw that it was true. Halverson was nowhere to be seen. If they tried to sneak down to the meteorite's resting place, it would be just like him to jump out of a copse of evergreens and arrest them.

Reluctantly, they crawled away from the hillside ridge overlooking the impact trough and made for their bikes. More than anything, A.J. wished they could have made it before the authorities, so they could have actually seen whatever it was that had fallen from the sky. But he wasn't about to tempt fate by pressing their luck with Chavez. Not with feds lurking about, with a certain Black Eagle logo on their car.

It was on their return trip to Jerry Flat Road that they came upon the same fishing lake they'd passed on the way to the impact.

The entire body of water was perhaps a hundred yards in diameter, thirty feet deep at its center. It was surrounded by a forest of reeds and short grasses, with tendrils of fog curling up from the ground. This time, however, A.J. noted the mist was much thicker across the entire lake surface than it had been on their way out.

"Hold up," he instructed, laying his bike to the side with a well-practiced unsaddling motion. "You see that?"

Molly wanted nothing more than to salvage the day. She was at his side in a hot second, scanning the water for whatever it was that had seized his attention. "What is it?"

"The water..." A.J. pointed.

Liam strode forward with purpose. "Holy shit, it's boiling!"

"What? Really?" Kris knelt by the shore of the tiny lake, watching a steady flow of bubbles from beneath the water's otherwise placid surface.

"I don't think so," A.J. argued, squatting and carefully dipping an index finger into the water. He retrieved it unscalded. "See? Not hot at all."

Liam pointed at the water, and A.J. immediately wiped his finger dry on his Levis.

"Look."

"I see. Something killed the fish."

All five friends stood on the lake shore, watching the small, silver-yellow bodies of countless lake perch drift lifeless just below the surface.

Chlöe retched as the smell hit her.

"This is in the path of the meteor," Kris proposed. "Maybe a chunk of it fell in the lake and killed the fish."

"Could be," A.J. nodded. "Let's poke around a bit. But if you see any sizzling rocks, don't touch 'em."

Liam and Chlöe wandered to the south end of the lake, while Kris and Molly headed north. A.J., wandered in a vaguely northeastern direction, lost in thought.

When the first flash happened, he thought it was perhaps distant lightning reflecting across the overcast sky. But then he heard movement, and saw the reeds and tall grass shift with the motion of bursting air. The noises were wet and slippery, and sounded like a wounded animal trying to escape capture.

Being the closest in physical proximity, A.J. trudged toward the disturbance, trying to see through the thick wetland vegetation. Whatever it was, it wasn't a raccoon or waterfowl—the thrashing was far too active, and large. Just as A.J. finished going through the options in his head and realized the possibility of it being a wounded cougar, the shape turned over in the grass and A.J. saw a face.

A human face, olive-complected, with graceful, feminine features and hair of emerald green. Then a twisting of limbs and the briefest flash of a patch on the shoulder of a zippered gray jumpsuit—a stylized Black Eagle on a white shield.

"Oh shit!" he blurted out in surprise, not realizing the person in the reeds was probably just as startled, just as frightened.

The others heard him, and began to make their way back to his location.

"What is it?" Liam hollered.

A.J. glanced at his friend momentarily, but when he turned back to his quarry, he smelled burning vegetation and was blinded by a familiar strobe of light. His ears popped as the air filled the now vacant area back in. Whatever it was, *whoever* it was, had vanished.

"It...it was a person," A.J. stammered. "It was human."

Kris probed into the weeds and grass, which was flattened into ruts that certainly looked as if someone had been dragging themselves out of the water and onto the shore. "What was?"

"Holy shit," A.J. blinked. "It was human."

"So you said," Molly quipped, running the toe of her Converse trainers over the ruts in the grass, revealing a shape singed into the wet soil at the end of the flattened reeds.

Liam peered over the tops of his mirrored aviators. "Well, well, well."

"Lookie there, A.J.," Molly smirked, fascinated. "Our sigil."

Sure enough, the broken triangle glyph was seared into the lake weeds like a brand, steam and smoke still wafting into the air. The total size of the sigil was a great deal smaller than the ones they'd used to teleport among the Old Town mines, Indian Bluff, and...whatever government installation A.J. and Molly had stumbled upon.

A tiny whimper escaped Kris' lips.

Chlöe hugged her arms around her slender frame and shivered. "This is creeping me out, you guys."

Kris squinted at the sky and realized the sun was already beginning to hang low. "It's gonna take us an hour to get back to town," he warned. "We probably shouldn't stay out here too much longer. You know...with the sheriff...and the feds..."

A general agreement arose in the form of everyone retrieving their bikes from the shore grass.

"Amazing," A.J. murmured, "just amazing."

Molly placed a hand delicately on his shoulder. "What did you see?"

"It was human," he answered, locking eyes with Molly. "Female, I think. And she clearly has the ability to teleport."

"Yeah?"

"Yeah, she blinked out just before you guys could get to see." A.J. bent down to pull his Huffy upright and straddle the frame. "And here's the thing," he added, nodding at the ruts near the lake shore. "She put that sigil there."

Track 22:
UP ALL NIGHT

Boomtown Rats (1981)

After the incident at the lake, the air seemed oppressive, and the whole valley seemed to close in around the river. Most of the gang scattered to their respective homes, arriving just as the sun fell beneath the Pacific horizon. Normalcy was the cure for what had become an ever-escalating series of mysterious events, and it seemed to be less and less effective as they grew accustomed to dealing with the ever-present dark.

Though smaller than Molly's basement, A.J.'s bedroom felt somehow safer at the moment, and he and Kris decided to stay there and brainstorm over some Jeno's microwave pizza rolls and Dr. Demento's syndicated radio show.

As the bathroom accordion of "Weird Al" Yankovic's *My Bologna* wheezed and growled in the background, Kris sat on the edge of the bed, a plate of hot snacks balanced on his knees. A.J. plopped down in a squeaky swivel desk chair and tried his best to explain his experience with the strange figure at the lake.

"She was a little taller than me, I think. Maybe Liam's height."

"You sure it was a girl?"

"Yes. Pretty sure. I guess. Shut up. And she was wearing, like, a gray flight suit."

"Wait, you mean like pilots wear?"

"That's what 'flight suit' would indicate. And the patch—"

"Was she cute?"

A sound of the purest exasperation escaped A.J.'s lips as he fumbled for a response. "Wh...what...does that even matter?"

"I think it would be cool to date an alien chick."

Another frustrated silence took over as A.J. pondered a reply to what was a pretty standard fourteen-year-old-boy statement. Prior to Molly and Chlöe hanging out with the guys and bringing a sense of maturity to their club, it was honestly a lot of dick jokes and farting on each other as an act of social dominance. Sometimes entire *D&D* sessions would go by without a single polyhedral die being rolled, so engrossed they were in discussions about which science fiction or fantasy heroine was hotter, and the merits of Tanya Roberts' nude bathing scene in *The Beastmaster*. Sometimes they'd kill a mob of walking skeletons, or slay a dragon. But usually it was about boobs.

"Dude, we don't know she's an alien."

"But the symbol is from alien writing..."

"Yeah, according to Time-Life Books, anyway." A.J. blew across the still steaming pizza roll in his fingers. "But her arm patch was the Black Eagle insignia Molly and I saw in the secret installation we teleported into."

Kris watched as A.J. opened his mouth to take a bite of the tiny pastry, knowing it hadn't cooled long enough. He'd grown up with Slavic pocket pastries and was an old pro at eating them. For a split second, he debated warning his friend, but A.J. was kind of being an über-intellectual dick today, so Kris said nothing.

A.J. bit into the pizza roll and immediately regretted most of his life choices as the molten magma of microwaved pizza sauce squirted out, instantly scalding his tongue, gums, and the roof of his mouth. "Sonnovabitch!" he cried, spitting out the un-chewed glob of food onto the paper plate in his lap. "Goddamnit!"

Kris tried not to smile. "Yeah, they're still pretty hot."

A.J. grabbed the open can of Rondo from his desk and took a healthy swig, letting the cool citrus work some of its healing magic. He finally swallowed it, and was immediately back on topic. "Either the government discovered this 'alien' language from one of the dozens of UFO crashes, like the one at Roswell...or what the public *thinks* is an alien language is *actually* a leaked government project."

"In teleportation..."

"Dude, it's the government. They're into some weird shit."

The sudden crash from the carport outside was followed by A.J.'s father bellowing from the living room. "Alan! The raccoons are back in the cans! Did you secure the lids like I asked?"

A.J. sighed, already rummaging through his desk drawer for a flashlight. "Pretty sure I did, Dad!"

"Doesn't sound like it! You and Kris go check it out, will ya?"

"Yeah, Dad! We got it!" A.J. nodded his head in the vague direction of "outside", and went to the door.

Kris set aside his plate of pizza rolls. They'd probably be edible by the time they got back from cleaning up the spilled garbage and securing the cans.

With greasy fingers and a single flashlight, the two boys traversed the short wood-paneled hallway at the rear of the house, and out what was essentially the garage door to the covered carport. A.J.'s flashlight beam roamed the contours of his father's silver '79 Buick Skyhawk, his mom's orange '77 VW Dasher wagon, his Huffy bike leaning against the side of the shed at the rear of the parking slab. No sign of disturbance, presently or otherwise.

As they rounded the hood of the Buick, however, they could see what had made the crashing sound. Both aluminum garbage cans had toppled over, spilling their contents onto the concrete and the adjacent planting strip where A.J.'s mom cultivated rhododendrons. At the base of the cans lay an unconscious human form—female, with the same tan complexion and gray jumpsuit A.J. had seen at the lake. Rubber-soled boots rose to mid-calf, and even her hands were encased in gloves of some sort of flexible space-age material. She was only exposed from the neck up, and A.J. noticed her androgynous haircut once again, tinted a light emerald green. If he didn't know differently, she looked as though she could have been the singer in a new wave band, or the model for a Patrick Nagel painting.

A.J. froze in his tracks and swallowed hard, his mouth still throbbing from the pizza sauce injury.

She was here.

At his house.

Why was she at his house? And who the hell was she in the first place? And how the hell did she get here?

His last question was answered when they approached the unsettlingly-still form of the stranger. An electronic device lay near her left hand, blinking brightly-colored LED readouts and settings.

"Dude, is that—?"

"Her?" A.J. answered Kris' question instinctively. "Yes. Yes, it is."

Kris squinted at the young woman. "She's got green hair."

"Yeah. So?"

"Nothing. It's just cool is all. Sara from my bio class has green hair. It's neat."

A.J. whirled, blinding Kris with the flashlight beam. His voice was a blistering stage whisper. "Kris! The color of her hair is irrelevant! We need to figure out what we're gonna do!"

Kris shrugged, batting the flashlight from his face. "I dunno. Tell your folks?"

"We're not gonna tell my folks. That'll open up the whole can of worms from earlier in the year."

"Aww come on, it won't be *that* bad—"

"We do not want my parents involved," A.J. insisted. "Trust me."

"Then we need to sneak her into your room."

A.J. and Kris paused, staring at each other, then turned in unison to look at the young woman splayed unconscious on the Jenkins family carport pad. Finally, A.J. took a deep breath and handed Kris the flashlight. "Okay," he huffed, kneeling next to the girl on the concrete and carefully retrieving the electronic device next to her hand. "Here, put this in your pocket."

Kris took the device, slipping it into the front pouch of his pullover hoodie.

A.J. maneuvered to her head, gazing down at delicate, almost elfin features. Noticing a nasty discoloration at her right temple, he nodded toward her legs. "You get her feet. We gotta be really careful. Looks like she's taken a hit to the head."

"Gotcha." Kris squatted down, gathering one of her legs in each hand and standing as A.J. lifted her upper body.

"She's surprisingly light," A.J. remarked as they angled toward the carport door.

"They probably don't have Pop Tarts and Jeno's pizza rolls on her planet," Kris offered.

"Dude. She's not an alien."

"We don't know that."

"Okay, we don't know she's an alien."

"We don't know she *isn't* an alien."

"Just shut up and get her to my room."

With dexterity and physical comedy in equal measure, the boys managed to wrangle the unconscious stranger across the short hallway into A.J.'s bedroom without drawing the attention of Mr. Jenkins, who had a direct line of sight into a section of the hallway from his armchair in the living room.

Once within the relative safety of A.J.'s room, they laid the girl gingerly on his bed, atop the sunset-striped white cotton comforter. Then Kris got to work calling Liam, Molly, and Chlöe, while A.J. got a cold compress and a glass of water, and went to tend his guest from a folding chair next to the bed.

By 8:15 p.m., the entire gang was reconvened in a bedroom with flower-print curtains and sci-fi movie posters, standing around a twin bed displaying the unconscious figure of a green-haired girl in a gray jumpsuit. Her head was turned slightly, the compress lying across her temple and forehead.

Chlöe might have been a little jealous of the group's attention, but couldn't help exclaiming herself. "Omigod, I love her hair."

"It's pretty rad," Molly had to agree.

"Like Sara in bio," Liam grinned, slapping hands with Kris in some masculine ritual of having had to be there.

"Guys," A.J. scolded. "Come on. I really don't know what to do here. What if the feds come looking for her?"

"You think she's a fed?" Molly pursed her lips in thought.

"She's got the insignia," A.J. shrugged. "Call it a hunch, but they'll probably want her back."

Liam agreed. "Yeah. Yeah, you're probably right."

"You say she just appeared in your carport?" Molly asked.

A.J. nodded, holding out a hand to Kris. "Yeah. Teleported. She had this on her."

Producing the electronic apparatus from his sweatshirt pocket, he carefully handed it to A.J., who turned it delicately over to look at the various readouts. The device was still alight with blinking displays and flashing characters, some of them resembling the "alien" language from Kris' Time-Life book collection. "I think this is how she travels."

"Careful with that," the girl warned in a fatigued tone. Green eyes matching the shade of her hair fluttered open.

Everyone stood back with a shared gasp.

The girl didn't move, but stared intently and earnestly at A.J. "Please," she urged. "I only have the one."

A.J. blinked. "You...you speak English."

"Almost as well as you." A smile broke across the girl's face, and A.J. felt his stomach flutter. She propped herself on her elbows and held out a hand. "Could I please have my key back?"

"Key..." A.J. repeated, eventually realizing she meant the electronic device currently in his possession. "What? Oh, this? Yeah." He offered the object back, and she accepted it with a slow blink and graceful nod, sitting upright against the headboard and gazing around at the room.

"I'm pretty sure this isn't a government facility..."

Kris jammed his hands into his jeans pockets and looked away as her eyes met his. "It's A.J.'s room, actually."

"And A.J. is...?"

"Me," A.J. raised a hand in a halfhearted wave.

"Hi, A.J." she sighed with a half-smile. "I'm Eren."

Every time the strange girl looked in his direction, he felt warm, and bit nauseous. His reaction was obvious to everyone else in the room—except Kris, who had the same response.

"I hope you understand," Eren said quietly, "that I have some questions."

"Of course," A.J. affirmed. "And, uh, so do we."

"Are you an alien?" Kris blurted from across the room.

Eren chuckled. "No. No, I'm not an alien." She shifted on the small bed and took a deep breath. Her tone suddenly turned serious. "I'm from Earth," she explained.

A.J. waited for the other shoe to drop, and his visitor didn't disappoint.

"Just...not this one."

Track 23:

STAND OR FALL

The Fixx (1982)

"**A** different Earth?" A.J. repeated with a heavy swallow. His chest hurt.

Liam leaned forward from A.J.'s desk chair in the corner, peering at his friend over the top of his aviators. "Dude—you totally called it."

"Dimensional travel!" Kris exclaimed in a stage whisper so giddy he resembled a cast member from *The Muppet Show*. "A.J. totally called it!"

"I just said that," Liam chided, launching a pencil at the back of Kris' head.

Eren sat up against the pillows on the bed, Chlöe standing by with a glass of water, which the visitor graciously accepted. "Thanks, um...?"

"Chlöe."

"Chlöe," Eren repeated. "Pretty name."

"Thank you," Chlöe blushed. "You weren't awake yet, but I was just saying how much I love your hair—"

Molly caught Chlöe's eyes and silenced her with a shake of the head and a "cut-off" hand signal.

"Guys, please?" A.J. interjected, his mind spinning like a laboratory centrifuge. "You seem about our age."

Eren's ability to keep calm and maintain eye contact was unnerving, but A.J. was gradually warming up to it. "Seventeen," she said.

"So what exactly are you doing here?"

Eren took a slow sip of water, letting it soak her tongue. She set the glass on the milk crate night stand. "That's a little complicated."

"We've had a complicated year."

The traveler's face suddenly fragmented into an expression of worry and paranoia. "What do you mean, A.J.? Did you encounter the first team?"

A.J. frowned. "First team? I...I'm not sure. We definitely encountered your teleportation sigils, closed a ley line nexus, and came face-to-face with more ghosts than I care to think about."

"Did you use the gates?" Eren asked, rephrasing for clarity. "The...sigils?"

"Did we!" Molly chuckled. "A.J. and I traveled to a secret government facility, with a UFO in storage, and that image on your shoulder patch..."

Eren shot Molly a look of wide-eyed discovery. "You were *there?* In the facility?"

"Yeah," Molly shrugged.

"You saw the ship?"

"I think so," A.J. replied, confused. "Looked kinda like a waffle iron."

Eren's face went blank. "I...don't know what that is."

"Round and flat," A.J. said, miming rough dimensions with his hands.

Kris rolled his eyes, dumbfounded. "Wait, you don't have waffles on your Earth?"

"That's what you're getting from all this?" Molly hissed at him. "Down, boy."

"If you've been inside the facility," Eren said softly, leveling a grim gaze at the teens around her, "then perhaps I can salvage the mission."

A.J. leaned forward over the back of the folding chair. "What mission?"

"This is gonna sound crazy to you," Eren warned, and her comment elicited an amused laugh from the group.

"Teleportation," Molly said.

"Ghosts," Chlöe added.

"Ley line nexus," Kris and Liam said in unison.

"Government agents," A.J. finished, a dramatic full-stop to the point being made.

Eren glanced down at her knees. "Yes, that might be a problem." She adjusted her posture, swinging her legs down to sit upright on the edge of the bed. "Okay, I'd better start at the beginning," she sighed. "I'm a pilot with the Cascadian Defense Force."

A.J. squinted through his thick frames. "What's that? Cas...Cascadian?"

"It's a bio-region in the Pacific Northwest. Used to be a province in the United Territories, before gaining independence after the economic crash of 1952."

Molly glanced around the room, noting everyone's absolute focus. A.J. stared in rapt attention as Eren continued her tale, the cogs and wheels turning in his head. He would have to write all this down someday—maybe sell the story to a science fiction magazine. "Your patch," he said, indicating his own shoulder. "Is that the CDF insignia?"

Eren looked at her own shoulder, then back at A.J. "Black Eagles are a special unit," she explained. "Named for a Shasta freedom fighter."

"We have the same guy!" Kris blurted out excitedly.

A.J. silenced his friend with a look, then turned back to Eren. "Why would a secret government agency on our Earth be using the same insignia?"

Eren shrugged. "Possibly because it's the only identifier we wear. Honestly, I don't blame them for being obsessed. If we had interdimensional travelers flying around in advanced vehicles on my Earth, we'd want to find out how and why they were there." She reached up to the bump on her temple and winced with the contact. "They really complicate matters, though," she added with another sigh.

"Your mission," A.J. urged.

Eren closed her eyes and nodded solemnly. "Right. Six years ago, an invasion force of unknown origin arrived. They've never actually been seen outside their battle armor, and encounters tend to be at a distance. We just call them Invaders."

"Wait," Kris interjected. "Aliens? Actual aliens?"

"We don't know," Eren frowned. "Upright bipeds with advanced space technology. Hive-mind. Their only communication with us has been through destruction. Bioweapons, in particular."

"Bioweapons?" A.J. mused.

"Yes. One of the first affected our population on the cellular level. Wiped out everyone over about thirty-eight. That's why we have seventeen-year-old Black Eagle pilots."

Molly gasped, and Liam grunted from the corner.

"Dude."

Eren ran a gloved hand through her mop of green hair. "It's not good back there right now. We're losing. Badly."

Chlöe pursed her lips thoughtfully. "Were you scouting for another Earth to escape to?"

A.J. raised an eyebrow. It was a good question.

Eren shook her head in the negative. "We'd developed a weapon. A delivery system for a micro-singularity that, if targeted on the command ship, could essentially wipe out their communications network and leave them leaderless. Took an insane amount of energy to make, and we just have one."

"So you were stashing it here," A.J. reasoned. "Not a bad plan, actually."

"The first team was sent to hide the weapon until we'd located the command ship," Eren explained. "But they were discovered and taken into custody. That's why I asked about the facility and the ship."

"We never saw any actual people," Molly said.

"Didn't expect you would," Eren replied. "If they were captured, they've disappeared deep into the well of government black ops facilities. Even if they survive interrogation, we'll likely never see them again."

"Does the ship we saw actually have the weapon?" A.J. asked.

Eren shrugged. "Won't know until I see it myself, but there's no reason to think the government agents would know what they were looking at." She leaned forward, resting her elbows on her knees, chin in her hands. "A second team was sent to retrieve the weapon earlier this year, but there were...complications."

"What complications?" A.J. asked.

"They surprised a couple of kids out by the old town, inadvertently teleported them into the facility. They managed to save the kids and send them back, but were caught themselves."

"Jeannie and Eric," Liam offered. A.J. shot him a look of agreement.

"Do you know them?" Eren asked, breathless. "Are they okay?"

"They're fine, far away from here," A.J. assured her. "So that explains the glyphs around Old Calico. Your soldiers were hiding out."

"It was close to the forest," she said, "where the facility is."

Kris scratched his forehead. "What I want to know is, why all the ghosts? In Old Town, up at the McCabe house..."

Eren nodded again, looking contrite. "When we travel, we use the natural ley line network to jump from place to place. Sometimes, a lot of travel can destabilize a local area, causing small tears in the space-time continuum. What you experienced were likely what we call *phantom leaks*."

"That's what happens to Kris," Liam quipped. "Every night."

Molly folded her arms across her chest and leveled a "mom" look at Liam. "Can you not?"

A sudden knock sent a jolt up every spine, and A.J. stood to man the exchange with his father through the bedroom door.

"Alan? It's getting late. Your friends should be heading home."

"I know, Dad. We're just finishing up the module. Won't be long."

"Um, okay then. Just keep it down to dull roar. We're going to bed."

"Okay, Dad."

There was a short pause, then A.J.'s dad signed off. "G'night."

"Good night, Dad."

A.J. returned to the folding chair and straddled it. "I'm not gonna speak for all of us," he began, meeting Eren's eyes with his own, "but I want to help you."

A general murmur of approval circulated from the occupants of the room.

"Looks like we're all in," Molly smiled.

Eren glanced around at each face. She'd been remarkably stoic up until that point, but their earnest goodwill made her eyes well up. "Thank you," she said softly.

"What do we need to do?" A.J. asked.

Kris looked suddenly concerned with the late hour. "Wait—we're doing this *tonight?*"

"As opposed to next week?" Liam spat. "Like you were doing anything else but going home to make wall-babies."

A.J. shot the other boys a savage look. "Guys. Knock it the hell off." He returned his focus to Eren.

"What are 'wall babies'?" she asked.

A.J. waved away the question with both hands and a mumble, trying to divert back to the initial question. "What do you need?"

"I'll need the power core from my ship," Eren explained, "and the nav card."

"That might be difficult. The impact site is swarming with police and government agents."

"Impact site? Oh...that's not the power core," Eren said with a wink, and A.J. found his stomach doing somersaults again. "That's the jump drive. When we punched through, something at the entry point damaged our ship. We jettisoned the jump drive to throw off the authorities, and ditched the ship in the lake." She looked at A.J. "Where you first saw me."

A.J. blinked. If they traveled the ley line network, and had "punched through" at the McCabe nexus, had he and his friends somehow caused an impediment by their sealing of the dimensional portal? He would have to see this through now.

"You said 'we'," Molly observed.

Eren's face dropped again. "My mission partner, Rej. He...didn't survive the crash."

"That's terrible," Chlöe offered. "I'm so sorry."

"I've lost my parents, siblings, my whole family," Eren admitted. "My Earth is in tatters. But you have given me hope of completing my mission, to save it. And for that hope, I thank you."

"So we get the power core from your ship," A.J. thought aloud, itemizing a mental task list, "then we get back to the facility, steal the functional ship with the super-weapon, you drop us back here, blink home, deploy it, *wham-bam-thank-you-ma'am*."

"Something like that," Eren said. "Maybe with a tweak here and there."

Liam stood from the corner desk chair and gestured a thumb toward the carport outside. "So let's saddle up and go," he grinned.

"You don't need bikes," Eren said. Removing her left glove, she pushed the sleeve of her jumpsuit up far enough to reveal a brand on her inner wrist—the broken triangle glyph. "This will take you to any reciprocal gate."

Molly's eyes widened. "You burned one into the reeds by the lake!"

Eren smiled, showing off the electronic teleportation apparatus in her hand.

"Does it hurt?" Kris asked.

"Only for a moment," Eren assured him. "Like a shot from the doctor."

A.J. recalled finding Jeannie at the bottom of the saloon sinkhole in Old Calico, and the brand she sported on her wrist.

It was all making sense now.

Molly and Liam were probably the only members of the group who, under normal cir-

cumstances, would have ever considered a tat-
too or some other kind of permanent body
modification, and only when a bit older. But
these were not normal circumstances, and
A.J. of all people found himself leading the
charge.

Pushing the left sleeve of his sweatshirt up
on his left arm, he extended his hand. "Let's
do it."

Track 24:
A MEANS TO AN END
Joy Division (1980)

A crackle of ozone and brief flash of light erupted by the north shore of the lake. Six human figures appeared in the misty reeds. Five immediately bent over to vomit on the ground.

"It takes some getting used to," Eren offered.

"Yeah," A.J. said, wiping his sleeve across his chin. "Been awhile."

The lake and surrounding grassland was dark and cloaked in mist, the pitiful light from a waxing crescent moon unable to pierce the cloud cover. Voices of both frog and insect were quiet tonight.

Eren took a quick appraisal of the group. Thumbing a button on the electronic key, she shined a bright LED element over the water's dark surface. Tendrils of fog clung to the top, the barest hint of movement beneath. A green frog croaked from the nearby grass and leaped into the water with a tiny splash.

"I'll need someone with me for this," Eren said, looking over the assembled friends again.

Liam took a hard breath, raising his left hand with purpose. "Let's rock."

"You're Shasta," Eren smiled, squinting at his tan, angular features.

Liam nodded, blushing. "Some, yeah. My mom's side."

"I'm Shasta too," Eren said. "Right on."

The way she said it so casually, and yet with a hint of interest, made him feel warm in his chest, and his guts wriggled like serpents. Maybe it was her attitude, her inherent likability. Maybe it was the natural pheromones of a seventeen-year-old girl. Maybe all of the above. Whatever her interpersonal gift was, Liam and his four friends were clearly on Eren's hook and willing to do anything she asked.

Turning her attention to the others, she relayed the plan: "Okay, Liam and I are gonna jump down into the ship. We're pulling some fuel, the power core, and a control console. Should take less than four minutes. You guys sit tight."

"I've never been inside the ship," Liam worried. "What do I do?"

"Just close your eyes," Eren said, placing her left hand gently aside his face. "I'll do the recall for both of us."

Suddenly they were gone, a close wind filling the void left behind as everyone's ears popped.

The ship's bridge was dimly lit in red emergency light and periodically flickered in showers of sparks. Water dribbled in a series of leaks from damaged seals, and the entire vehicle was pitched at a downward angle with its nose in the ancient silt and mud. It was round and open through the center, with a couple of workstations and control panels on either side of the main view port. The port itself was an actual window, about eight feet across, revealing nothing of the outside environment in the form of swirling, murky gray-black. Padded swivel seats sat atop metal arms that jutted from the deck.

The body of a teen boy with Eren's tan complexion and green-tinted hair lay splayed on the deck under the pilot's station. A wide smear of blood traced a line from the point where his head hit the floor to where the ship, and his body, had come to rest.

Liam's knees unlocked and he immediately lost his balance on the canted floor. Eren steadied him, and he eventually found his bearings.

"Easy there, soldier," she smiled.

Liam swallowed the bile in his throat, indicating the dead body. "Is that...?"

"That's Rej," Eren nodded. "He was my mission partner."

"I...I'm sorry."

Eren placed a strong but gentle hand on each side of Liam's head and locked eyes with him. "It's okay. I have a lot of friends to mourn when this is all said and done. But we've got a big checklist ahead, and I need you to cowboy up for me."

She winked at him, patted his right cheek, and disappeared toward the flight workstations.

Within seconds Liam was standing—though still wobbly—on the deck, while Eren pulled cowlings off components and cover plates off control systems.

"Go to the aft section," she instructed, leaving Liam somewhat confused.

"It's round," he said. "Where's 'aft' on a saucer?"

Eren popped up from under the flight control workstation, which looked as if it was hemorrhaging wires and cable harnesses. "Oh. Yeah. Solid point." Pointing with some kind of cable-cutting tool in the general direction opposite the main viewport, she added: "Over there, in the compartment marked *JUMP FUEL*. Pull three canisters, would you?"

Peering over his mirrored shades, Liam staggered along the uneven deck toward a section of the ship that definitely had more of an "engineering" look to it. As promised, a storage unit resembling a slender-profile refrigerator was labeled *JUMP FUEL,* and it was stacked with yellow metallic cylinders, black handles extending from the ends.

Clutching a handle in each hand, Liam pulled the canisters from their housings, grunting as they swung toward the floor. "Whoa!"

"Yeah, they're heavy," Eren admitted, appearing from the dark with a translucent green computer card that resembled some kind of arcade game circuit board.

"I won't be able to carry all three," Liam warned.

"That's okay," Eren assured him. "Just clamp the third one between your legs until we get back—someone else can carry it." She flipped a clear cover from the engine console near the fuel storage, grabbing a red-handled component and twisting it in place. It unlocked, and she removed it from the housing. "There's one last thing," she added, heading back to the navigation console and punching up a dialog on the work screen.

Liam saw a flash of computer code, and then a series of red numerals counting down seconds. His eyes widened and his throat went dry. She had set a self-destruct countdown.

"Let's go," Eren said casually, turning to face him. "Think of the lake shore and touch the brand."

Liam hesitated, caught in a moment of brain lock.

"I'll wait for you to jump," Eren assured him. "But we need to go *now*, or we're going to be compressed down to a more...*subatomic* size."

"Right," Liam blurted, shaking the cobwebs from his head. Still holding both fuel canisters, he visualized the shore of the lake, and the glyph burned into the reeds. He brushed a fingertip lightly across the raised brand on his inner wrist, and there was a blast of light and the whoosh of air returning. Liam was gone.

CR

Liam dropped both fuel canisters in the tall grass, leaning over to release the meager contents of his stomach onto the ground. The third fell backward from between his calves. Eren blinked into view moments later, flash accompanied by a localized boom as the air pressure shifted.

She handed the power core to A.J. as he took stock of the two travelers.

"You get everything?"

Eren nodded. "Power core, nav card, and enough fuel for three jumps."

A.J. hefted the metal cylinder in both hands, silently doing the math. He reckoned she meant one jump to get them out of the installation, one to get her ship back to her dimension, and a spare for contingency.

The surface of the lake suddenly buckled, erupting in a fountain of bubbles as the volume of water below shifted to fill the void where the ship once rested.

While Chlöe took one of the fuel cells from Liam's hand, Kris took custody of the one in the grass by his feet.

As Kris stood, feeling its weight, he spotted the strobe of red and blue from a police vehicle light bar in the distance. Hissing to get Molly's attention, he cocked his head toward the path that wound along the south lake shore.

"Uh, guys," Molly warned. "Looks like Chavez is up late."

Eren saw the flashing strobes and turned to face A.J. "You remember the facility? What the inside looked like?" Her eyes locked with his, and he felt his fear and trepidation melt away.

A.J. nodded, and the Bronco pulled closer to the lake.

"Okay, everyone hold onto A.J.," Eren instructed, and immediately everyone encircled him, grabbing hold of a belt loop or a collar. With the weight of the power cell heavy in his right hand, he was nonetheless able to brush an index finger across his wrist.

Sheriff Chavez pulled to a squeaky stop just inches from the lake and popped open the driver's side door. Was that a lightning strike she'd just seen? She grabbed the roaming spotlight on the door and shined it in a thick beam across the lake, but it revealed only darkness, and the mist over the water.

Track 25:
MATTER OF TIME
Berlin (1980)

Six travelers arrived in a dark chamber, crowded within a column of light from the illuminated symbol in the floor to a dim gray light in the ceiling. It was of course the same room A.J. and Molly had visited on their experimental journey back in June.

Eren peered past the light into the distance. "This the place?"

A.J. nodded, swallowing dry air. "Yep."

Nudging him in the ribs, she urged, "It's all you, buddy. Just get us to the ship."

As the teens dispersed from the light into the dim space beyond, they saw the chamber was not nearly as cavernous as it had appeared from within the column. A.J. led the group toward the exit, urging quiet and discretion.

"Okay, there's a door here," he whispered, flashing back to the epic dungeon crawl adventures he'd narrated for his friends over the past year. "We're gonna go left, down the hallway. Straight shot to the door at the end. That's where the ship is." He shot Eren a brief look of disclaimer. "Or *was*, when Molly and I were here."

Eren nodded, satisfied with the warning. There were no guarantees, and these kids had already brought her far beyond where she'd have been able to go on her own. "They probably wouldn't have moved the ship unless they knew you'd been here. Our chances are good. Let's just keep quiet and get to the ship as fast as we can."

Chlöe glanced at Liam, who winked back. His sass and bravado had seemingly returned.

Molly and Kris both gave a thumbs-up.

A.J. took a deep breath and nodded, reaching for the door handle.

∞

Corporal Parkinson wasn't sure what all the commotion was about. Something about there being a big development with Project Black Eagle, and suddenly the whole Siskiyou base was on alert. He just knew his leave had been cut short, and he'd been tasked with guarding the research installation on middle watch, from zero-hundred to zero-four-hundred. He just had two hours to go.

As he poked his head inside the telechamber, something cylindrical and incredibly heavy rocketed out of the dark. There was a hollow *thunk*, a jarring white flash, and his vision closed in. Corporal Parkinson landed in an ass-plant on the floor, splayed out against the opposite wall, unconscious.

"Holy shit," A.J. wheezed, standing over the limp body of the soldier in his black BDUs and the Eagle insignia patch on his shoulder.

Molly flashed a grin, stepping out into the hallway. "Good one," she whispered.

"Hey," Eren whispered from behind A.J.'s head, "that's the only power core we have, so...y'know...try not to bludgeon too many people with it."

"Right," A.J. nodded, still in a state of moderate shock.

"This way?" Eren pointed to the left.

"Yeah."

Molly was already out in front, her body surging with adrenaline as she caught sight of another soldier flipping a plastic cover from a wall panel and slamming a hand on an alarm button. Suddenly the already dim lights within the installation flashed red, and a klaxon erupted from loudspeakers in the ceiling.

"Shit!" Molly hissed.

Kris huffed up beside her, lugging the fuel cell under his arm. "Guess we failed our stealth roll?"

"Botched," Molly answered. "Natural one."

Every moment brought them closer to the soldier, who approached the door to the hangar, hand on his sidearm holster.

"We just have to fight it through," Liam growled. "Like the orcs at Ravendeep!"

Then he was out in front, screaming a teenage war cry, surging forward at the head of the group like the vanguard of a barbarian army.

Eren shot A.J. a brief look of confusion. "What's Ravendeep?"

"Tell ya later," was the hurried reply, and then everything was chaos.

The soldier stood ready at the end of the hall, next to the hangar door, fumbling with the snap on his holster. "Stop!" he warned. "Hold it right there!"

Someone else shouted "Halt!" from the hall behind them. A.J. didn't look back, but knew they would be sandwiched between angry government agents if this didn't go extremely well in the next couple of seconds.

Chlöe went low, slamming her fuel cell into the side of the soldier's knee, causing him to lean to the side as it collapsed beneath him. His pistol shot went wide.

Liam came in from the soldier's left, swinging his fuel cell from the handle like an odd sort of baseball bat. The soldier's head snapped to the other side, and his pistol skittered across the corridor. He slid down the wall, landing in the same ass-down display as Corporal Parkinson.

Eren arrived at the door and was surprised to see no electronic security. It made her nervous. "Not even a card scanner?" she mused.

"I think the security in this place is all on the outside," A.J. said.

Molly opened the door into the hangar as a chorus of shouted warnings approached from the hallway behind them.

Eren and her five companions were through in seconds, and she latched the door shut from the inside. Shifting the control card to grip between her knees, she reached to the small of her back and produced her electronic "key" device that had provided the teleportation brands they all sported. Pressing a single button on the handle, she aimed it at the seam in the doorjamb where the latch mechanisms intersected. A brief orange flicker and a beam of light, and suddenly the door was held in place by a bubbly mass of rapidly-cooling molten metal.

"This won't hold them for long," she warned, as the sounds of boots and angry epithets approached the door. "Let's get to the ship."

A.J. scanned the cavernous room. It was much the same way he and Molly had left it, in that they'd merely peeked in and hadn't touched anything. The salvaged ship still occupied the center of the space, round and modern, like something from a Syd Mead art book.

Eren pressed another control on her device, and a hatch opened in one of the flattened, blocky segments along the outer circumference of the saucer. There was one each at the twelve, three, six and nine o'clock positions, twelve o'clock being the main view port. A small ramp extended down the few feet necessary to hit the concrete floor, and Eren waved them in. One by one, the teens scampered aboard, looking around at the science fiction interior that encircled them.

It was much the same as Liam had experienced on Eren's crashed ship, though slightly larger, with a circular column in the center which seemed to be made of translucent white plexiglass.

Eager to show off his edge in experience nonetheless, Liam immediately headed aft to the engineering section, popped open the fuel compartment, and stowed his canister within. "Fuel over here, with me," he ordered, as Chlöe and Kris hurried to repeat his actions. "A.J. Power core, back here."

Liam flipped open the transparent cover and helped A.J. heft the heavy cylinder into the receptacle. When A.J. let go, Liam twisted the handle, locking it in place.

Eren slotted the control card into the main console, and pressed a few buttons and toggled switches. Suddenly all the consoles came alight with flashing neon colors, and the column at the center of the ship began to glow. She turned in her chair to examine the pulsating blue-white light and smiled in satisfaction.

"Looks like the jump drive is good to go," she announced. "Everyone take a seat and strap in. We're getting out of here."

The banging at the hangar door was replaced by the slow, inexorable crash of a handheld battering ram.

"They're breaking through the door!" Chlöe exclaimed.

Eren flipped some more switches, and a sudden, sub-sonic rumble erupted from the engineering section, escalating in pitch as the ship began to rise slowly off the concrete. She turned to A.J., indicating the workstation to her right. "Come sit next to me—co-pilot's station."

A.J. blinked, unsure of himself, but definitely not in favor of surrendering to the federal authorities presently breaking through the door. "What do I do?" he asked, sliding into the padded chair and strapping in.

"Nothing just yet," she said, turning to her left. "Everyone else find a station. We are leaving."

Molly found herself at a workstation with several back-lit buttons indicating direction and a single red one that seemed to be some kind of fire or launch control. The view screen in front of her showed the far end of the tech bay, including the segmented garage door at the far end.

Eren examined her own screen, noting various statistics as they flashed by. "Somebody on one of the weapons consoles, target that bay door and fire."

Molly immediately thought of the buttons on the *Asteroids* cabinet at the diner, and how well she'd done at keeping Liam from reclaiming his top score spot. "I'm on it," she said, manipulating the bright red reticle over the steel door with the left four buttons. She managed to get the target somewhat centered, slapping her right hand down on the red fire control.

Bright crimson light swelled within the groove on the top of the fuselage, shooting outward around the roof of the ship, meeting at a point near the main viewport. Where it connected, it swelled again, and a beam erupted from the point of light. The laser shot forward, carving a massive chunk of segmented door and blowing it into the forest outside.

As the battering ram made a final impact and the tech bay suddenly filled with scientists and black ops military personnel, the captured vessel from an alternate dimension cleared the access door and shot away into the forest without so much as a blast of thrusters.

Eren's eyes were alight with hope. "We got the ship, you guys!"

A *whoop* of triumph went up from the group, and Molly's face almost couldn't contain her grin.

"Did you see that shot?" she bragged. "I'm pretty awesome."

Liam huffed, strapped into a chair at a second weapons console. "Damn, girl! Gimme a chance to catch up!"

"You'll each get the chance to shoot down some bad guys," Eren cautioned, and A.J.'s stomach fell through the floor.

"Wait. What? Aren't you taking us home?"

Eren frowned, confused. "Well...yeah. Of course. But I need your help first. We're not done."

"Hold up," A.J. protested. "The deal was we'd help you get the ship."

Eren found his eyes, and he noticed hers were welling with tears.

"I still need to deliver the weapon," she said, a quiver in her voice none of them had heard before. "Without you to man the weapons and defend the ship, I won't be able to get to the coordinates—they'll kill me. This is my Earth's last shot." She punched up a screen on her console and turned her attention back to navigation.

"Please, A.J.," she begged, fighting back the quiver in her voice. "I need you."

The saucer careened low over the wetlands south of the Rogue River, a gray ghost in the dim light of the crescent moon. It banked right at the river's mouth, rolling gracefully on a smooth edge, angling north toward the hillside above Calico.

"Yo, dude," Liam scolded from the weapons station behind A.J. "We are not bailing on Eren. Not now. I will seriously kick your ass if you say otherwise."

"Yuuup!" Molly agreed, screwing her face into the human equivalent of a Wrong Way road sign. "Who else doesn't want to go to a different dimension in a flying saucer to save the world—show of hands?"

A.J. bristled at the attack, but said nothing. Kris and Chlöe, however, piled on.

"I can't believe you'd pass this up," Kris frowned.

Chlöe sighed in clear disappointment. "Really."

"Okay!" A.J. protested. "I'm in! I'm in! Jeez!" He sheepishly fiddled with the buckle of the safety harness on his seat. "I was just clarifying the plan."

Eren smiled, blinking away the water from her eyes. "Thanks, A.J."

"It's just..." he muttered, "I've never been to another dimension before..."

A collective gasp of tired exasperation erupted from the ship interior. Molly's eyes rattled back in her head and she almost screamed.

"Seriously?"

Kris shifted in his seat at another weapons console. "Um, hey, so has *nobody*. Except Eren."

"It's okay," Eren assured the group, pressing some keys on the console as Timber Hill loomed large in the viewport. "Approaching the jump point."

"Oh, wait!" A.J. cried suddenly, and Eren banked the ship away and west, toward the Pacific Ocean.

"What! What is it?"

"You said something damaged your ship when you came through last time. I think that was us."

"What do you mean?"

A.J. winced. "We...we closed the nexus back in October."

"Oh yeah," Molly frowned. "Shit."

Eren took a deep breath. "How...how did you *close* a ley line nexus?"

"Vinegar and sea salt solution," Kris explained.

There was a long pause as Eren took the ridiculous information on board. Did chemistry and physics really work so very differently here? Finally, she opened her mouth to respond, though better of it, and punched in a new set of navigation coordinates. "There's another nexus over Mount Shasta. We can be there in a few minutes." A quick 180-degree pivot set the saucer on course over the Rogue River-Siskiyou National Park.

"That was smooth," Chlöe commented, referring to the ship's movement. "What does this thing use for fuel, anyway?"

"Good question," Molly chimed. "Were we swinging around plutonium back there?"

Eren kept punching in flight coordinates, not looking back. "It's a gravitic engine," she explained. "We use dark matter."

Kris wrinkled his nose. "What's that?"

"It's what comes out after you eat too many microwave burritos," Liam sighed. "Don't you know anything?"

Molly cocked her head, peering over Eren's shoulder at the navigational display, deciding it better to simply ignore Liam. Her hands were shaking in anticipation of traveling to space, let alone space *in another dimension*. "What's dark matter?"

"I've read about it," A.J. said.

Chlöe chuckled. "Of *course* you have."

"It's supposedly like eighty-five percent of the matter in the universe, but about twenty-five percent of the mass."

"Very good," Eren admitted, impressed. "Gold star for you, A.J."

"Yesssss!" A.J. hissed, pumping his fist in the air. "Gold star!" For a brief moment, he thought himself asleep in his bed. This was clearly a bizarre dream. Not even the kids in

E.T. had been able to go onto the spaceship at the end. His mood elevated a bit, until Eren made her next announcement:

"We're over the Klamath Forest," she said. "Coming up on Shasta. And it's gonna get a little hairy."

"Hairy how, exactly?" Kris asked.

"You'll feel the nausea of the jump, to begin with. But we'll be in enemy airspace almost immediately, and they'll be on us in a second or two." Eren swiveled in her seat to face the others. "I'll concentrate on flying us to the delivery coordinates, but the four of you at those gunner stations will have to keep their drones off our back."

Molly, Kris, Chlöe, and Liam each took a moment to caress the illuminated buttons on the console. Gizmo's in Gold Beach mostly had stand-up videogame cabinets, but Kris had been to an arcade in Medford with a sit-down version of *Star Wars*. The targeting screen reminded him very much of the brightly-colored wireframe display in the game, which had swallowed many quarters.

A.J. cleared his throat a bit too conspicuously. "Um, what do I do?"

"You get to deliver the weapon," Eren said, catching his gaze with a brief wink.

He swallowed, but his mouth was dry.

"Shasta ahead," Eren warned. "Here we go."

The saucer careened toward the massive mountain peak at Mach-5, vanishing into a burst of lightning. An endless carpet of evergreen trees waved and jostled in the rush of air filling the sudden void.

Track 26:
NO WAY OUT
Missing Persons (1982)

Ears popped and stomachs retched as the ship reappeared over the volcanic mountain in a blast of white light and a thunderous sonic boom. Despite the dizziness and nausea, all aboard miraculously avoided purging onto the deck plates.

The saucer banked into a roll, shooting toward the upper atmosphere at high velocity. Inside, the travelers sank into their seats, reacting to a mere fraction of external G-forces. Molly found the sensation akin to the corkscrew segment of the Demon, a rollercoaster at Marriott's Great America she'd visited with her parents the previous year.

Eren set the throttle at maximum, and the ship blasted out of the thermosphere with another jump that made every gut tingle as if going over a steep hill in the backseat of a car. A million pinholes in a vast curtain of black shone with twinkling points of light, the great sliver of a crescent moon visible in the distance.

Chlöe glanced nervously out the forward viewport. "Are we in space?" she asked.

"Close," Eren said quietly. "Exosphere."

"I hardly felt those Gs," Liam remarked, swiveling in his chair.

Eren turned briefly to face him. "You wouldn't have. Part of taking a vehicle this large through a jump is keeping it within a *gravisol* field."

"Sounds like a cream for athlete's foot," Molly chuckled, hearing the chunky guitar riff from Jim Carroll's *Wicked Gravity* in her head.

"Gravitic isolation field?" A.J. posited, getting another stomach-warming smile from their green-haired traveling companion.

"You got it. That's why we still have limited artificial gravity, even in zero-G environments, like space."

A.J. gasped in mock excitement. "Does that mean—?"

"*Two* gold stars." Eren nodded. She reached in front of A.J. and punched a couple buttons which instantly illuminated, along with a tactical grid on the video display.

"Okay, eyes on the drones. Tell us where they're coming from."

A.J. shot a self-satisfied smile back at his friends. "*Two gold stars!* Ha!"

The guttural sighs of exasperation and matching eye-rolls were universal and immediate.

Then the saucer bucked and jerked sideways from impact, and A.J. found himself looking at several glowing blips on the screen.

"Uh oh! Looks like ten...uh...enemy ships?"

Eren nosed the ship into another corkscrew maneuver, frowning. "Where?"

A.J. imagined the traditional clock display over the ship icon at the center of the sensor display. "Um, four o'clock? Right...er, *starboard* aft quarter!"

"We're still three minutes from delivery coordinates," Eren announced. "You guys keep them off us!"

Kris, Chlöe, Liam, and Molly instantly sprang into action, moving target reticles and pounding their FIRE controls.

As the saucer flipped over in a lateral roll, a formation of scarab-like craft swarmed from behind, shooting out of the atmosphere in their wake. Red light circulated in rings around the saucer's top groove, coalescing in four different points of laser fire.

The first drone broke apart in a silent, sparkling explosion, cut in half by the beam of light. Liam let out a joyous whoop of victory, imitating Chekov's Russian accent from *Wrath of Khan*.

"*Got heem!*"

Molly's face showed no sign of being impressed. "Great kid, don't get cocky."

Fanning out, the beetle-shaped drones opened fire, pelting the saucer with charged particles, causing the ship to buck and shake again.

"Damnit, guys," Eren huffed, "keep 'em off us!"

Molly slammed her hand on the fire control, and another drone flew apart.

On every screen, neon-colored wireframes careened around like an angry insect swarm. Kris longed for the small wheel control of the *Tempest* cabinet at Gizmo's arcade, but made do with the illuminated joystick regardless.

Another target lock, another burst of crimson light, another drone blown apart, its robotic components spinning off silently into the void of space.

Another, and another.

Within moments, all ten had been dispatched, and the teens in the saucer breathed a collective sigh of relief.

Suddenly a red light flashed on A.J.'s console, and his eyes grew wide behind his thick glasses. "Uh oh." He scanned the display screen, calling out the warning. "Second wave —dead ahead!"

All eyes adhered to the monitors, reflecting flashes of neon blues and greens. A literal wall of drones stretched laterally to each side of them, impossibly long.

Before A.J. could speak, Eren hauled back on the throttle, then nosed down and punched full ahead into a screaming dive. The drones followed, flexing solar-cell "wings" and spewing an endless stream of charged particle ammunition.

They were everywhere. There were too many of them. Impossibly many.

Kris was just making that exact complaint when Liam suddenly had an epiphany.

"Guys! It's *Galaga*!"

Chlöe squinted. *"Galaga?"*

But Molly was already a mile down the track. "It is! It's 3-D *Galaga*!"

"Exactly," Liam smiled, lining up multiple drones within a single silhouette in the target lock and slamming a hand down on the fire control. The saucer emitter erupted in a point of red laser light that shot out into infinite space, and an entire line of drones silently shattered into component pieces. "Line them up, multiple targets! Double fighter, baby!"

"It's more like *Space Invaders*," Chlöe shrugged, eliciting a chuckle from Liam.

"Ha! Not even, dude."

A frustrated groan went up from Molly's gunnery station. "Does it matter? Just line 'em up and knock 'em down!"

Infinitely long spikes of crimson light flashed from points around the neon ring atop of the saucer, cutting through lines of drone fighters, silently sending pieces adrift in empty space.

But they kept coming.

As soon as a rank of six or eight drones were punched through with a beam of laser light, another filled the empty space.

Eren strained at the flight controls, putting the ship into a reverse of the original corkscrew maneuver, as it bottomed out of the dive and shot back up, bringing the drones drafting behind. "Almost at the delivery coordinates," she informed A.J. through clenched teeth. "Get ready. Green switch on your right. The one that says *DEPLOY S-P-C*."

Then the invader command ship appeared just a hundred klicks distant, looming out of the blackness of space. A.J. glanced up at the main viewport and shuddered in fear.

"Hol-ee shit," Kris marveled, catching a partial glimpse of the thing. "Big boss!"

A.J. couldn't disagree. It was colossal, a craft larger and more complex than anything he'd ever seen in a short lifetime of science fiction films. Crab-like and bristling with sensor antennae and weapon platforms. Pulsing with amber and red waves of light, it was the mother of all mother ships.

"A.J.? Come on, don't freeze up on me now!"

Blinking and willing himself awake from this terrible dream, A.J. returned his attention to the monitor display in front of him. Four triangular arrow-points pulsed neon green toward a center point. He saw the blips on the screen appear as a seemingly endless swarm of new drones swelled from housings on and underneath the command ship's fuselage.

The arrows converged. A tiny alert rang out from the console. The saucer shook and shuddered with impacts from behind.

"A.J.!" Eren cried. "Now!"

The first two fingers on his right hand pressed down on the glowing plastic button, and for a brief moment the interior lights and screens on the saucer all dimmed and brightened in unison.

A microscopic ripple in space-time ejected from the top of the saucer, a tiny warping of the star field, instantly tracking toward the massive spaceship.

The center section of the command ship imploded, crushing in on itself as adjacent sections and modules floated away, trailing an intermittent strobe of sparks and drifting smoke.

Instantly, the glowing eyes on a hundred scarab drones went dark. The sentries floated lazily in chaotic dispersal, occasionally impacting one another.

"Holy crap," A.J. muttered. "Did we do it?"

Suddenly Eren's face filled his vision and before he knew it, she was planting a firm kiss on his lips.

Four voices joined together in a jubilant cheer, becoming howls and laughter.

Eren pulled away, a rosy blush to her cheeks for the first time. "Thanks, A.J." she offered quietly, adding: "Thanks, you guys." She saluted, then spun back to face her piloting station. "And now I'll get you back, before I have to report in."

Throttling forward again, Eren took a deep breath and sighed.

"They are not gonna believe me when I debrief."

"Just tell the truth," A.J. said.

"Yeah," Liam chimed in. "You met the coolest teenagers in any dimension and they saved your Earth with superior hand-eye coordination."

Eren let a genuine laugh escape her throat, and Liam melted into his chair.

Stomachs lurched again as the saucer rocketed back down to re-enter the atmosphere. Eren angled the round ship, cutting through the friction as flames seared the outer shell.

A warning light flashed bright on her panel.

"Uh oh," she warned. "Power cell was damaged. I'm at thirty-six percent."

A.J. looked at her with concern. "What's that mean?"

"I won't be able to jump from Shasta," she said. "If I'm gonna get home, I'm gonna have to go through the Timber Hill rift. It's closer."

"But we closed it," Molly frowned.

A.J. nodded in agreement. "Isn't that what damaged your last ship coming through?"

"We don't know that," Eren scolded. "And I don't have time to argue. If we're all gonna get home, I need to make the jump from Timber Hill."

And that was all there was to it. No sense in arguing the point. Shoulders tensed. Stomachs flipped and wriggled as gravity—real gravity—made itself known again.

The ship plunged down out of the night sky like a falling eclipse, black and round in the soft gray haze of the new moon. Unlike their Earth, there was no Calico, no sleepy riverside community nestled in the last meandering curve of the Rogue. No lights winked from glass windows. No one lived here.

A flat hilltop beckoned from above the crop of evergreens near the water's edge. There was no creepy abandoned mansion here, no endless parade of specters.

Eren flipped a switch, there was a mechanical lurch, and the hillside lit up with houses. Even in the middle of the night, there were considerably more points of incandescent light dotting the community along the north bank of the river.

A.J. realized he'd been holding his breath from the last time Eren spoke, and he let it out, relieved. Until a shrill alarm klaxon sounded from Eren's console, and she spun in her chair, unsnapping her safety harness with her right hand, and pressing a combination of control buttons with her left.

"Dammit," she growled under her breath.

"What's wrong?" A.J. queried, genuinely concerned.

"Everyone get on the deck," she ordered, and harnesses were immediately shucked. She met their eyes, and it was the gravest look they'd seen. "I need you guys to hold onto A.J. and recall his room."

A.J. knew the ship was in trouble, and she was effectively telling them to bail out. "But there's no return sigil—"

"There is," Eren assured him. I branded the floor under your bed just before we jumped to the lake."

A.J. started to speak. "Eren—"

"Please," she gulped back a sob, corralling her fellow travelers onto the deck in a tight grouping. "There's no time. Just do this. And thank you."

Five bodies shoved together, and A.J. closed his eyes and thought of his bedroom, with the flower print curtains, and the milk crate night stands.

He ran a finger softly across the raised brand on his inside wrist, and in the next instant, they found themselves standing in the center of the small suburban bedroom, some on the floor, some on the bed.

Kris burped foulness from his upset stomach, and leaned over to gag and retch into the wastebasket next to A.J.'s desk.

The knock at the door was aggressive and louder than before. "Alan? It's two in the morning! Come on now! Time for your friends to go home!"

A.J. shook the dizziness from his head. "I know, Dad!"

"Now, Alan! I mean it!"

"They're going, Dad!"

"Okay then."

Just as the group had recovered from the shock of teleportation followed by instant parental disapproval, lightning flashed within the room and ears popped as the air pressure shifted again.

Eren knelt on the floor, head lowered, body wracked with quiet sobs. A single canister of jump fuel clattered to its side on the floor beneath her huddled form.

A.J. was by her side immediately. "Eren? What happened?"

It took a few awkward seconds to compose herself enough to form a coherent answer. Her eyes were red-rimmed and wet with tears as they gazed into his own.

"I had to ditch the ship," she began, still gasping and shuddering with every breath.

The room went absolutely silent as five curious minds began to make connections and figure out what it all meant.

"The power cell was blown and I didn't have enough to get back to the jump point. I had to set the destruct and jump here myself."

A.J.'s heart sank on her behalf. He knew her next words before she said them.

"I'm stranded here."

Track 27:
SPACE AGE LOVE SONG
A Flock of Seagulls (1982)

Christmas ended up a drizzly, dreary affair, but the group gained a new member when Liam's "long-lost cousin" Eren turned up in town with the clothes on her back and a well-crafted, believable story about her father's abuse and alcoholism.

Liam's mother took her in on a temporary basis, with the understanding that she would contribute toward the grocery bill, and A.J.'s mom, who happened to manage the Val-U Drug on Third Avenue, engineered a Christmas miracle. Eren had a part-time cashier job there within seventy-two hours, and was a minor community celebrity within the first week of 1983.

Chlöe presumed it was because of her cool hair. And everybody did love the hair, to be sure. But A.J., Kris, and Liam—and even Molly to a certain extent—fully understood her way with people. Her higher-vibration, dimension-hopping, planet-saving, vulnerable-yet-unknowable, very human magnetism.

Registering for a half year of high school seemed a futile gesture, so Eren put in more hours at work instead, and began to get various papers and identification in order. A social worker at the Quartz Valley Reservation in California helped her secure a tribal ID, which she parlayed into a Social Security card, and an Oregon driver's license.

She eventually sweet-talked Gary at the auto shop into selling her his non-starting '77 El Camino, which she had repaired and running two weeks later. It became a group project car, a labor of love shared at first by Liam, then eventually the rest of the posse. In a month, they had tricked it out with a new dual exhaust and swapped out the stock transmission for a Turbo Hydra-matic. When it was completely painted and detailed the week following that, Eren began to give Bodhi a run for his money as the coolest kid in town. The Reynolds family Volvo just couldn't hold a candle to the metallic-black custom light pickup with white stripes and gleaming chrome.

And yet, Bodhi could find no fault with this absolutely likable newcomer. Having just turned eighteen himself, he became her biggest fan, and Chlöe was so busy tending her own girl-crush, that she forgot to be jealous.

Not that there was anything to be jealous of.

Eren never dated. Not from the group, nor from the community, though A.J., Liam, and Kris all tried at one point or another. She let each boy down without souring their friendships or injuring their pride, placing the emphasis on her requiring emotional solitude for this period of adjustment to her new surroundings.

Molly took her cue from Eren when it came to keeping the group dynamic a platonic arrangement. She felt a close kinship with each of the boys on a different level: Bonding with Liam over music or videogame competition, boosting A.J.'s spirits whenever he spiraled into self-doubt, and keeping her physical crush on Kris absolutely silent. Perhaps, eventually, she'd reconsider her self-imposed prohibition, but for the time being, all parties were satisfied with how it was.

By the time school ended in mid-June and everyone gathered to watch Bodhi walk at his graduation, it was as if Eren had always been in Calico. Like she was meant to be there.

She was a lively and integral part of the group, a chaperon to R-rated movies like *The Entity* and *Videodrome*, and an occasional companion for A.J.'s epic *D&D* dungeon-crawl adventures, where she played a convincing cleric, smiting the undead, and healing the other party members. She became a big sister and den mother to the gang, a mentor and beloved friend.

The warmest of the summer weather arrived in late July, and with it the camping season. Many nights were spent on the river bank, or tucked away at the group's secret spot in the woods up by Miller Creek, off Highway 515. The nights were cool, the days were sultry and smelled of pine.

Then, as the dog days of summer arrived, Eren began to disappear. She never showed anyone exactly where she went, but she told the gang about a spot she'd found further up the mountain, near Rock Creek. A.J. was worried at first, as they'd all noticed a gradual malaise settle over Eren like a tiny personal storm cloud.

When he caught a glimpse of a shimmering phantom from his bike as he rode to Molly's one August morning, it struck him as odd. The luminescent form of a Buffalo Soldier in uniform wafted silently in the breeze as the ghost made its way onto Pioneer Avenue from Baker Street. It took no notice of the boy or the bike, nor did A.J. pursue to investigate further.

Just the same, it was an indication that the local network of ley lines had been reawakened. And it troubled him something awful.

He only mentioned the sighting later, after the gang had convened to watch *The Secret of NIMH* on the Reynolds family's new Betamax player, and stuff themselves with pizza—which Eren adored, and was able to metabolize with superhuman efficiency.

A.J. knew the report would cause concern, but he wasn't prepared for the look of abject sorrow from Eren. She remained silent for the rest of the evening, and A.J. lay awake all night, wondering what that silence meant. Then he revisited a familiar internal battlefield, kicking himself for his initial cowardice at the prospect of traveling to Eren's dimension, especially since she'd done just fine being marooned in his.

They celebrated the last golden days of summer with a fishing trip and cookout on the river, with a proper campfire and a dual-cassette boombox that blasted Molly's mix tapes to anyone in the local vicinity who cared to listen to Wall of Voodoo and Talking Heads. She'd gotten even better with her mixes, usually building them around a theme, like *Songs About Planes;* or a band, like *The Cure For All That Ails You,* or *Police Brutality.*

Eren was notably touchy-feely, hugging everyone and having one-on-one conversations about how special everyone was to her. She even shared a beer with Sheriff Chavez when she dropped by to check in on the kids.

Chavez had been charmed months ago upon their first meeting, thus there was no citation for underage drinking. Not even a warning.

Every internal alarm in A.J.'s psyche was triggered. Everything about Eren's demeanor and actions screamed finality.

He was absolutely terrified.

Finally, A.J. approached Eren as she cast a few more lures on the river. The sun began to sink orange and gold in the western sky, limning her face in a warm, ethereal glow. Her hair had gotten longer, a mop of black roots fading to green, pulled back under a rolled bandanna.

"What's going on?" he asked quietly.

She didn't look at him, but watched her line bob in the water. "Thank you, A.J."

"For what?"

"For *what?* For helping me complete my mission. For helping save my Earth. I will never forget you guys."

A.J. put a gentle hand in the crook of her elbow. "Eren, what is it? Really."

"I went back to the facility," she admitted, still observing the ripples around the float in the eddy where the hook dangled below the water's surface.

"Without us?"

"It's been shuttered."

There was a short pause as A.J. took in the new information.

"Like..."

"Like mothballed." She finished his thought, finally glancing momentarily in his direction, never shrugging away from his gentle contact. "Without the ship, they've got nothing. So they closed up shop. At least that's what I assume."

"Wow," A.J. sighed. "But why did you go without us?"

She smiled wistfully. "I'm sorry, man. You'd already done so much. Helping the mission, taking me in, helping me survive here...I felt like I should scout it out myself."

A.J. nodded, and she closed her eyes as a soft breeze came in off the river.

"Anyway, I managed to locate a few components. And with the jump fuel I grabbed from the ship, I was able to send a message back. To my world. To let them know I'm alive, and...to send a rescue when they can."

"Did this happen when you went up to your spot up by Rock Creek?"

She nodded, letting a simple, "Mmm," vibrate across her pursed lips.

"Do you know when they might come get you?" A.J. asked, swelling with tears he willed behind a stoic wall of concern.

Eren shook her head and took a deep breath, beginning to reel in her line. "I'll get a signal on my key," she explained, and A.J. remembered the small electronic device she used to brand teleportation sigils on people and places.

"So not a lot of advance notice, then."

"No," Eren said, a tear trailing down her sun-kissed cheek as she finished reeling the lure and turned to face A.J. "It's best that I just disappear. Don't tell anyone until after. You can let the gang in on it, but tell everyone else I went to live with relatives in Montana."

There was a long silence as A.J. and Eren watched the sun shimmer on the river in a fiery golden dance.

"I'll miss you," he said quietly, finally unafraid to look her square in the eyes.

Eren dropped the fishing pole and wrapped A.J. into a tight, loving embrace that seemed to last an eternity. The up-tempo, sax-laden groove of *Fear to Fear* by Romeo Void filtered into A.J.'s ears, and he caught himself smiling at the lyrical relevance:

Take me with you

Please don't go alone

I don't wanna think of you

Out there so low

Every word of that, he thought, as her lips bussed his ear.

"Write this all down someday," she urged. "I mean it."

"No one'll believe it," he chuckled, inhaling the scent of coconut sunblock and river breeze from the hollow of her neck.

"That's why they call it *fiction*," she smiled, finally pulling away to look at him once more. "But *we'll* know better."

They returned to their friends, and neither mentioned a word of what had transpired between them.

The fish fry broke up at sunset, Sheriff Chavez taking her cue from Judas Priest grinding out *Breaking the Law* on the boombox. She wished the kids the best of luck in their new school year, reminding them to pack out their empty cans and trash as she revved the Bronco and sped away onto the frontage road.

At about 4 a.m. the following morning, Liam awoke to a silent flash of lightning outside in the yard.

A quick check revealed Eren's room to be vacant. Returning to his own bed, he found an envelope taped to his door. On it was delicately scrawled:

Liam—For when you get your license. Thanks for everything—E.

Within it was the pink slip for the El Camino, with the registration signed over to him, and a bill of sale for one dollar.

The group met at the diner for a last celebratory breakfast before the new school year began. Molly would be joining them at Calico High ("Go Lumberjacks!"), and Bodhi was preparing to head off to UCLA.

A.J. knew the moment he saw Liam that it had happened.

She was gone.

Gathering his friends in the large corner booth, A.J. filled them in on what had occurred, where she'd gone, and how it was ultimately for the best. They raised small glasses of orange juice and ceramic coffee mugs in a toast to their interdimensional friend, and their incredible year of adventure.

When Sheriff Chavez and Deputy Halverson entered talking about how the fire spotter at both Pyramid Rock and Brushy Bald look-outs had "reported multiple lightning strikes in the area, up near Rock Creek, and strange-ly, here in town just before dawn," A.J. let a smile creep across his face.

After breakfast, Bodhi drove everyone up Highway 515 to Eren's Rock Creek campsite, where A.J. found the empty jump fuel cylin-der, the Black Eagle insignia patch from her flight suit, and a teleportation glyph seared into the forest floor.

The patch would end up on the chest pock-et of a denim jacket in A.J.'s closet which would be outgrown by the end of sophomore year. Eventually the sleeves would be re-moved, and the garment would become a vest worn over a variety of hoodies.

The Calico Kids remained vigilant, though no phantoms were ever seen again around town. School returned, and with it came a comfortable blanket called normalcy. After the year a certain five friends in southwestern Oregon had experienced, the normalcy blanket felt good. Warm. Safe. And the friends shared it like they would the roof of a sleepover pillow fort.

But when the fall colors arrived in the Rogue River valley, when lightning arced across the sky and ears popped from changing air pressure, A.J. would slip Molly's *Bad Hat*

Harry mix tape into his Sanyo personal cassette player and climb onto his bed, feeling the autumn breeze through the flower-print curtains.

As he lay, smelling the pungent mixture of pulp mill, fish cannery and ozone, he'd slide the foam-covered headphones over his ears, cue up A Flock of Seagulls' *Space Age Love Song*, and think of his green-haired dimension-traveler.

The End

ABOUT THE AUTHOR

Todd Downing's love affair with genre storytelling dates back to his consumption of classic radio dramas and comic books as a child in the 1970s, which broadened into a general appreciation for sci-fi and fantasy media of all kinds.

He grew up in the greater San Francisco Bay Area, writing and drawing from a young age, his works ever-present in school literary journals and newspapers, and eventually on film. He married his high school sweetheart and moved to Seattle in 1991 where he began to write professionally, and worked as an artist in the videogame industry until his publishing company became a full-time operation, while raising two children amid the chaos.

Downing is the primary author and designer of over fifty roleplaying titles, including *Arrowflight, RADZ, Airship Daedalus*, and the official *Red Dwarf* RPG. He continues to write genre fiction for stage, film, comics, audio, and adventure gaming products.

Widowed to cancer in 2005, Downing remarried in 2009 and currently enjoys an empty nest in Port Orchard, Washington, with his wife, a pair of rescued cats, and a flock of unruly chickens.

Join the author's mailing list:
www.todddowning.com

Thrilling pulp adventure!
www.airshipdaedalus.com

Read the adventures of the
Airship *Daedalus:*
A Shield Against the Darkness
(Book #1)
Assassins of the Lost Kingdom
(Book #2, by E.J. Blaine)
The Golden City
(Book #3)
Legend of the Savage Isle
(Book #4)
The Arctic Menace
(Book #5)

Plus:
AEGIS Tales
A Retro-Pulp Anthology, Volume 1

Primordial Soup Kitchen
A Collection of Short Strangeness

AVAILABLE NOW
in ebook and print!

Made in the USA
Columbia, SC
22 September 2020